"So, what do you say  **up on the Mayans t** **he asked, already pi** **control.**

"I vote for *Snowfall*. I need to see what Franklin has gotten into now. Plus, we're like three episodes behind, and I need my Damson Idris fix."

Nick snapped his head toward me again, somewhat jokingly, but kind of not. "All right, no Damson ogling tonight, please. Especially when your handsome boyfriend looks nothing like him."

"Yes, but my handsome boyfriend picked lasagna over me tonight, so I don't think he gets to say what ogling does and doesn't happen," I responded, playfully pushing him.

"Oh, the dagger...in my chest... Someone help take it out."

"Okay, okay. Enough." I rolled my eyes and sat back into the corner of the couch, placing myself in our usual position for TV watching.

Nick clicked the TV to our shared Hulu account, pressed Play on the episode and jumped up to turn the lights off. When he returned, he took another bite of lasagna and then sprawled his body over my lap just as the opening scenes began. I placed a bet in my head for how long it would be before I heard his familiar deep breaths and soft snores. An hour, tops, I figured. And then, like clockwork, I'd tell him to go to bed, clean up the living room and eventually join him upstairs. Same routine as always. Loving as hell, but absolutely no spark.

Dear Reader,

If you're anything like me, some of your closest family members started off as friends. In fact, while I have two biological sisters and a brother whom I am very close with, you'd likely think I grew up with several more. And you wouldn't be entirely wrong—some of my friends I've known twenty to twenty-five plus years, so "sis" and "bro" naturally fall off our lips at this point. They are the people who challenge me and make me laugh so hard I could cry; they are some of my biggest champions and the ones who have held me as I've broken down in tears.

These relationships helped inspire *Bloom Where You're Planted*, the second book of my Friendship Chronicles series for Harlequin Special Edition. It's a sexy but introspective story about Jennifer Pritchett, a young woman who loves her boyfriend, '90s R & B and her friends—but lately, not much else. Like many of us at times, Jennifer finds herself comparing her life with those of the very people who want the best for her, and from her perspective, it's pretty lacking. But when she leans into these relationships for inspiration instead of competition, she realizes that everything she wants is right in her grasp, even the desire she craves from her partner.

Get ready to join back up with some of your favorites from *The Shoe Diaries* as they continue to navigate the ups and downs of love, their careers and their friendships.

Hope you enjoy!

Darby Baham

Bloom Where You're Planted

DARBY BAHAM

HARLEQUIN
SPECIAL
EDITION

HARLEQUIN®
SPECIAL
EDITION™

Recycling programs
for this product may
not exist in your area.

ISBN-13: 978-1-335-40858-7

Bloom Where You're Planted

Harlequin Enterprises ULC
22 Adelaide St. West, 41st Floor
Toronto, Ontario M5H 4E3, Canada
www.Harlequin.com

Printed in U.S.A.

Darby Baham (she/her) is a New Yorker of five plus years who has had personal blog posts appear in the *Washington Post*'s relationship vertical and has worked in the communications industry for more than two decades. Originally from New Orleans, Louisiana, she lived in the Washington, DC, area for fifteen years, where she cultivated a beautiful sprawling shoe closet and met some of the best people in her orbit. Her debut novel, *The Shoe Diaries*, was released in January 2022.

Books by Darby Baham

Harlequin Special Edition

The Friendship Chronicles

The Shoe Diaries

Visit the Author Profile page
at Harlequin.com for more titles.

To anyone who finds themselves comparing their journey to those of others, I hope this book helps to remind you that you are exactly where you need to be and who you need to be right now—even if your best is still yet to come.

Part 1

"Sometimes, all you can do is smile and move on with your day, hold back your tears, and pretend you're okay."

—Anonymous

Chapter One

"God, you're beautiful."

Nick's words came out as a whisper but rang in my ears like the sweetest piano note. In the middle of fumbling with his keys to unlock his apartme~ door, he stopped abruptly, turned in my dir~e. and stared at me with the slightest smile ~ *right* Looking like he wanted to tear my ~ *hear him* in his hallway. ~ *der my front*

"What was that?" I aske~e. say it again. I curled m~ ~*eautiful to meeee."* teeth and gave him ~*oothly as Joe Cocker*

"You, Jenn P

He sang th~

himself, and I about melted as he stepped closer to me and nuzzled his head in my neck.

With all the willpower I could muster, I stood firm, taking in the scent of his Tom Ford beard oil while desperately wanting to kiss those lips that had been mine to do with as I pleased for the past three years.

The only problem was that we'd just spent the past five hours on a brewery tour in DC, and I hated beer. The last thing I wanted to do was taste the remnants of it on his lips.

"You are so silly," I said, attempting to defuse the moment. "We should get inside before one of your neighbors catches you trying to seduce me."

"I don't care about them."

"I know you don't…right now."

The truth was that Nick didn't much care about anything in this moment, since he'd been drinking for me and him for the past few hours. I'd tried to ᵇa good sport and taste as many beers as I could ma¹ʰᵇ but inevitably I ended up pouring my re-
the tou ion into his cup to finish at each stop on boyfriend being. And my dear, normally very composed Tacs in my purs n he'd probably planned on hops in my mouth.
"Mmm, okay," he g I always carried Tic raised his head up so that h the aftertaste of the door. I watched Nick as he
d then

task and leaped his five-foot-ten-inch body over the threshold as his door swung open. We slipped off our shoes as we walked in—mine, a pair of nude-colored pointed-toe Vivienne flats that showed just a peek of my toe cleavage, his a pair of black leather oxford shoes with rubber soles and a tan trim from Bevana—giggling as we stumbled in the dark before turning on the foyer light.

Within seconds, he made a beeline for the bathroom, practically knocking over his charcoal-gray side table lamp on the way. For my part, I knew which room was most important if I was going to enjoy the rest of the evening: the kitchen, to get him some water. Stepping onto his tile floor with my bare feet, I braced myself for the cold but was pleasantly surprised that it wasn't as jarring as I expected. Maybe the little bit of beer I'd consumed had warmed me up more than I realized, or the slight breeze of early September in DC hadn't quite cooled down his apartment floors. I worked my way effortlessly through his space, knowing every nook and cranny as if it were my own.

From the cabinet above his island, I grabbed two drinking glasses and then slid over to the refrigerator to get his water pitcher. Just as I'd taken it out, Nick came bouncing toward me.

"Aht, aht," I said with one hand in front of me, stopping him in his tracks. "Before you come over here with those lips ready to kiss me, you need water."

"I also gargled some mouthwash while I was in the bathroom. Because I'm a loving boyfriend."

"Oh, yes, very loving," I laughed, rolling my eyes. "So loving that you're also going to drink this full glass of water. Not just for my tastes, but also to make sure you're not throwing up later and yours truly doesn't have to play Mom all night."

"That's fair."

Nick stood with his lip poked out, pouting like a little kid waiting for a treat that he'd been promised. It was almost comical watching him follow me as I took every meticulous step—rinsing each glass with water from the faucet, slowly pouring water from the pitcher into one and then the other, and walking back to the freezer to get ice with my long, wide-legged tan linen trousers causing it to almost look as if I was gliding across his floor. By the time I handed him his glass, his bottom lip was starting to quiver with anticipation.

"Is it considered cruel and unusual punishment if your girlfriend slowly tortures you when you're in need?"

"Why, whatever do you mean?" I asked with a teasing eyebrow raise.

"You know what I mean." Nick paused to take in a few desperate sips. "If you could have taken twenty minutes to pour that water, you would have."

"Maybe," I chuckled. "But I have to get you back for today somehow."

"You really didn't like it?"

Nick finished his glass, clanked it down onto the counter and moved closer to me, pulling my waist into him with one hand and using his other to run his fingers through my pixie-cut hair.

"I liked spending time with you, of course."

Instinctively, I melted into his body. It was something about the way he touched me, about the hold he'd had on me from day one. Whenever he directed my limbs to do something—lean into him, walk a few steps with his hand gently pressed on the small of my back, bend over so that my butt was in perfect position for him to slide into me—I sank right into him without warning. It was like my body had a mind of its own, and Nick controlled it. Tonight was no different. Even after purposely dragging out how long I took to fix him some water, as soon as he pulled my waist toward him, I completely liquefied in his presence.

"But—" I hesitated, not wanting the rest of my words to sound like a rant, but also needing to be honest with him. "The thing is, you know I hate beer. I mean, there are a million tours we could have tried. I'm not saying I don't appreciate the thought. I'm just saying it didn't seem like plans you'd make for a girlfriend who would much rather a tequila soda."

"I hear you. You're right. I just thought I'd try something different. I don't know, man."

Nick took a step back from me, and suddenly it felt as if a football field of space was smashed between us. *That was definitely not what I wanted.*

Just that fast, my limbs had lost their support beam, and me and my body felt the lonely side effects of honesty.

"You know what? How about we figure out something to eat?" I asked, anxious to fill the awkward silence and to get us back to the flirty, sexy place we were just in moments ago. "I could go for Mexican. You?"

"Oh, yes." Nick's eyes lit back up at the suggestion and the change of conversation. If there was one thing I knew about my boyfriend, it was that he hated conflict, so I was sure that he was all too happy to move on from my statements as well. "Let's get delivery from Alero, babe. Those nachos. Yum."

Even for him, this was sort of whiplash, but I'd take it.

"Okay, perfect. I was also thinking about their seafood soup."

"Ooh, and their carne al paso." Nick threw his head back with excitement.

"Yesss, that, too."

"Do you mind placing the order, though, babe?" Nick asked, his demeanor completely now switched back to where it was before—so much so that he started bouncing around again. I could always tell how good a mood he was in by how many *babe*s poured from his lips. Two in a row surely meant we were back in business. "Just use the app on my phone," he said, twitching some more. "I—I think I need to go to the bathroom again."

Ohhh. Well, that would also explain the bouncing.

"Ha, sure, leaky. No problem."

With fresh springs in his legs, Nick leaned toward me and placed the softest kiss on my lips. Right at the same time, he grabbed one of my butt cheeks for emphasis and then went racing back out of the kitchen before I could say another word. His physical affection was one of the things I adored about the man, but the beer I tasted on my tongue was not.

"And maybe rub some of that mouthwash on your lips, too?" I called out to him.

"Okay, Mom!"

It wasn't long before Nick joined me in his living room and plopped down on the sofa in between my slender legs. With his head falling somewhere in between my chest and stomach, I could feel the rhythm of his breathing as he inhaled and exhaled and a slight tickle on my skin from his goatee.

"Did they say how long it would be?"

"Yeah, probably thirty to forty minutes." With the fingertips of my right hand, I stroked the top of his head softly, alternating between figure eights and straight lines in his short hair.

"Mmm. Okay. Sounds good." His voice lowered to a whisper, and I knew he'd be asleep way before that time was up.

"You have a preference on what we watch tonight?" I asked.

"Nahhh," he said, dragging out the word and closing his eyes in the middle of his response. "You can definitely pick." By the time the last word came out of his mouth, it was barely audible through the yawn that accompanied it.

Once his breaths turned into light snores, I knew I was on my own until the food came. At least his arms were wrapped tightly around me, his broad shoulders contracting while the rest of him was calm. That, somehow, helped to reassure me that he might have gotten today completely wrong, but even his sleeping body knew that he needed me. The real question was whether I was happy with us as we were now.

With three years behind us, I knew in my heart that Nick was the man I wanted to spend the rest of my life with. We'd met, as many young adults do in DC, at a networking happy hour for up and coming Black professionals. It wasn't even something I'd wanted to attend—not much need for teachers to network with finance bros, as far as I was concerned—but I'd let my friends drag me out that night, and thankfully so. I'd just stuffed my face with a forkful of macaroni and cheese and chicken when this very fine brother walked up to me smoothly and introduced himself. I don't even think I ever took a second bite.

From then on, we were practically inseparable, talking on the phone for hours like we were kids in high school. I wasn't really the girl in our crew who dated a lot, but by the time Nick and I went on our first date two days later, then our second the next day and our third by the end of the week, even I knew we had something special. For the past few months, however, as much as I knew our love was strong, our connection felt off. The spark was gone. I'd feel a flitter of desire between us, and then poof, just as it came, it would be over. My body would be searching yet again for its lighthouse, but by then, Nick would check out and just want to sleep. And we'd find ourselves back on the couch, just like tonight, with me watching TV and him asleep between my legs. Were we just past that exhilarating and passionate point in our relationship now? Was this what long-term relationships looked like? I wondered.

It's not like I had a lot of examples to look to in times like these. I'd grown up surrounded by Black married couples in Sacramento, California, but I could tell most of them had stopped liking each other eons ago—you just didn't get divorced in my family; that was a definite no-no. My parents were a little better—still married after forty-five years and now retired, they spent the bulk of their time traveling around the world and laughing with each other. That was certainly something I wanted, but I hadn't seen my dad look at my mom with lust in his eyes maybe ever. And I wanted the desire in my relationship, too. Just thinking through those questions sent a wave of sadness over me. Maybe it was just inevitable to feel like Nick and I were stuck in a rut three years in?

It's certainly possible that it was me, too. It wasn't

like I exuded passion and desire lately, either. Once the energy starter of my friend group, I'd also seemingly lost my mojo just as my closest friends were doing things like dating a prince, suddenly quitting her job and getting promoted to run her office's IT department. Even my boyfriend, who grew up as the middle child of five boys in a lower-middle-class Black and Filipino home in the Bay Area, was now second in charge in his accounting department. And me? I was turning thirty in a few months and still just a third-grade teacher, erasing crayon from the school walls before heading to happy hour to meet my best friends every week. Talk about being the boring friend/girlfriend of the bunch.

Before I could go further down my rabbit hole of self-pity, I heard Nick's doorbell ringing.

"Baby, food's here." I shook him slightly to jolt him awake.

"Mmm." He continued lying there without moving an inch.

"Great acknowledgment, Nick. But I need you to move off me so that I can answer the door or get up so that *you* can answer the door."

"Right, right. Okay," he said with a sigh and slowly raised his body off mine. Wiping his eyes open, he walked to the door, dragging his once springy but now sluggish legs along the way. When he reached the door, he grabbed the food and gave the delivery guy a fist pound as thanks. He was back next to me on the couch within a blink, all with his eyes still barely open.

"I'm so excited for this food, but that nap… I could have slept all night right there."

"Ha-ha, yeah, you were definitely knocked out."

"Did you get to rest any?" Nick asked as he began tearing open the brown paper bag on the coffee table and pulling out the various to-go containers.

"Uh-uh, no. I didn't."

"Too much on your mind?" He spread out our full dining order on the table: steak nachos, shrimp quesadilla, seafood soup and the carne al paso meal that came with sirloin steak, El Paso garlic sauce, rice, fried yucca and salad.

"Yeah, I think so."

I wasn't sure how to tell him that he was one of the things.

"You want to talk to me about it?"

Nick looked up at me, his gentle eyes staring into my soul as he awaited my answer. Maybe the smell of the food had finally woken him up.

"Maybe. I don't know." I hung my head in shame. "I don't want to sound like I'm always complaining."

"And I don't want you to feel like you're alone."

Nick finished spreading everything on the table and turned to me, kneeling on the floor so that his arms were wrapped around my legs as he looked up to me. He stroked my thighs in comfort for emphasis. *God, I love this man.* This was why, even without the passion and desire that I craved so much lately, I couldn't see my life without him.

"Honestly, it's more of the same. Worried that I'm not really using my psychology and English degrees, tired of working in the classroom but unsure of what else I want to do, and just generally feeling like everyone's leaving me behind." I took a deep breath before continuing. "And then I think, Jenn, you're falling into the trap of being the sensitive one again. You're overthinking everything. And my worry bounces back and forth between those two."

Nick listened intently and then stood up in front of me, pulling me into a standing position, too, and enveloping his body around me. Then he bent his head slightly and kissed my forehead, letting his lips linger on my temple just a moment longer than he needed to in order to finish the kiss, but the perfect amount of time I needed to feel his presence.

"I love that you're the sensitive one. Yes, you are the kind of person who wears her heart and everyone else's on her sleeves. And maybe that's a heavy burden sometimes, but it's also what makes you loving and compassionate. It's why the kids at your school love you. It's like…" Cutting himself off, Nick moved to face the food spread on the table.

"It's like this seafood soup," he continued. "It's not as famous as steak nachos, and it doesn't get all the glory of the entrée, but *this*. Seafood. Soup. Right. Here?!" Nick pointed to the soup after every word to emphasize his point. "Once you have this soup, you can't get food from Alero again without it. It's just that good. And it makes you feel all warm inside and…"

"Okay, okay," I stopped him before the analogy could really get out of hand. "I get your point."

"Do you?" He stared deep in my eyes.

"Yeah, I think so."

"Okay, good, because now I'm extra hungry, and I feel like the soup is getting cold even as I talk about it."

"You're right. It's definitely time to eat."

Nick ran back to the kitchen to get bowls, plates and silverware for us to eat with as I settled back into the couch, happyish for now. By the time he returned, I'd already started picking up pieces of nachos and stuffing my face.

"Really, Jenn?" he asked, catching me midstuff.

"My bad," I mumbled out of my very full mouth.

"Guess that just means I get more soup!"

Nick sat back down next to me and lifted my right thigh onto his. We each grabbed our portions and began spooning them into our bowls and onto our plates. Nick's plate filled up quickly as he piled meal after meal on top of each other. I didn't really like my food to mix on my plate, so I had about a spoonful of each item as a first serving.

"Do you remember the first time we went here?" I asked.

"How could I forget? It was our third date, right?"

"Yeah, third or fourth. I was so nervous, because

at that point I realized that I really liked you, but I couldn't figure out if you felt the same."

"You mean besides the fact that we were on our third date?" he questioned, taking a huge bite of steak at the same time.

"Well, yeah, besides that," I said, chuckling. "But you could have still been feeling me out. I knew by then. And then we got there, sat down, and the first thing you did was drop all the silverware on your side of the table onto the floor."

"I was extra nervous. I somehow managed to meet a super smart woman who was from California, like me, in DC of all places. I wasn't trying to mess that up."

"Well, I thought it was so cute. Here was this extra confident, very handsome guy sitting across from me…and he's just as nervous as I am? You went up three more notches in my book."

"How many notches am I up now?" he asked with a wink.

"I stopped counting when I reached a hundred in the first couple months."

"Dammmmn. See, I knew I was a good boyfriend. But that's Hall of Fame–type stuff right there."

"Okay, don't get beside yourself." I playfully pushed him away from me.

"Nah, nah, just admit you've got a good one right here."

"I've certainly got a hungry one, that's for sure," I

said, pointing to his empty plate that had been filled and devoured once already.

"I'm a grown man, Jennifer. I like to eat." He raised an eyebrow at me, signaling he wasn't just talking about the food on his plate.

"Yes, I do seem to recall eating being a favorite pastime of yours," I replied, biting my lower lip and raising my eyes up at him.

With my right hand, I dragged my fingertips across the back of his neck, which prompted Nick to swiftly put his plate down and pull me fully onto him. Facing him with my legs straddled around his waist, I leaned my whole body into him and took his lips into mine. Nick took the cue and wrapped his arms around me while we hungrily took turns intertwining our lips and tongues. With fire in his eyes, Nick grabbed my hair and pulled my head back so that he could bury his face in my neck, alternating between bites and licks as he made his way down my jawline to the top of my white tank top, where my breasts poked out ever so slightly. Maybe the spark wasn't dead after all.

Just as my breathing became heavier with excitement, Nick yawned. Loud and long. Full on into my chest. *Well, so much for that.*

"Still tired, huh?" I asked, desperately hoping he would say no and keep kissing me.

"Yeah, I guess so." He sighed and picked his head up to look me in my eyes. "Can we table this until

I've gotten a little more sleep? I think it'll be better for both of us."

"Of course. I'm not going anywhere." This time, I kissed him on the lips to reassure him.

"Thanks, babe. I think I'm actually going to head to bed now. The exhaustion is really hitting me."

I peeled my body off his and watched as he stood up from the couch and began walking toward the stairs to his loft bedroom.

"You coming?" he asked, looking back across his left shoulder.

"I'll be up there shortly. Just want to put the food away first. Maybe finish watching this old episode of *Being Mary Jane*."

"Okay, cool," he said with another pout. "Just don't take too long. You know I can't sleep well without my Jenn blanket."

"Ha-ha, I know, Nick. I won't."

I watched him as he disappeared up the steps, climbing two at a time until he was no longer there. Then, I took a deep breath, steadied myself from the tinglings in my body I'd just been feeling not more than five minutes ago, and began picking up the dishes and containers from the coffee table.

Back in his kitchen, I washed our dishes and placed them in the drying rack next to the sink, stacked the leftover containers in the refrigerator and made sure to close the trash bag tightly after I threw away the bag everything came in. The last thing we'd want was to wake up to the smell of old seafood when we got up tomorrow morning. Using a dry towel, I wiped down the sink when I was done, making sure not to leave a trace of water. It was something my grandmother taught me growing up and was embedded in my brain now: your kitchen wasn't truly clean if your sink was still wet.

Lastly, I turned off the kitchen light and walked back to the living room. I grabbed the remote control and unpaused the TV as I sat down. My memory of the episode came back to me instantly. "Oh, yes," I said aloud. "This is the one where Mary Jane tells the guest on her show that they may have ideological differences, but they are both women fighting to be heard and seen. Hmm, well, I can definitely relate to that."

Two episodes later, I finally clicked the TV off and made my way upstairs to Nick's bedroom. He was in a deep sleep on his side of the bed—the right side—and facing the door, so I could see the expression of peace on his face. Undoing the fabric belt around my waist, I walked to the dresser that held my night scarf, all while slipping my pants off my body. I tied the satin scarf around my head, careful to keep my edges inside, and then grabbed one of Nick's T-shirts to replace the tank top I had on. I carefully unbuckled my bra and slid his shirt on, then folded up my clothes and placed them on his side chair in the corner of the room.

Tiptoeing so as not to wake him up, I walked to

the bathroom to wash my face and brush my teeth before bed. Nick's his and hers double counter made it easy for me to leave some of my bathroom essentials at his place: face wash, toner, moisturizer, even my electric face-cleansing brush. But I was convinced he was also using some of my stuff when I wasn't there, because it seemed to go down much faster at his place than at my apartment.

Once I was done with my nightly routine, I walked back into his room and climbed into bed, draping the covers over my body as I did. As if by instinct, Nick's arm sprang out and pulled me to him so that we were in a tight spoon position.

"I love you, Jenny," he whispered into my ear.

"I love you, too, Nick."

"And I'm sorry about today. I hate knowing it was that awful for you." He was half-asleep and obviously still thinking about what I'd said in the kitchen. This was why I rarely said anything negative to him. I never wanted him to think I didn't love and appreciate him. Full stop.

"It's okay, Nick. Honestly. I'm just… I don't know. It wasn't awful. It just wasn't what I expected." I sighed.

"Okay." His arms tightened around me, and he wrapped his legs around mine and nuzzled his head on the back of my neck. "We'll try again next weekend, okay?"

"Okay, babe." I closed my eyes and breathed in his

scent again, allowing my body to once again be enveloped fully by his. This was it, where I loved being.

But a pesky lonely tear inched down my face as I felt myself start to fall asleep.

Chapter Two

"Okay, so I've got these for our time at Meridian Hill Park on Saturday."

Reagan climbed out of the mess that she was making in her shoe closet, a pair of multicolored Coach loafers swinging from her fingertips.

"Ooh, those are cute," Rebecca responded, practically falling over as she craned her neck to check out the details of the shoe.

"And what do you have planned for the Spy Museum?" I asked, stuffing my mouth with a handful of nachos.

Reagan dropped the loafers in front of us and ran back into her closet.

"I'm thinking my white Chucks," she yelled from

inside, her voice slightly muffled as she pulled them from their place on her shelves.

"Okay, okay, so the only thing left is something for dinner Saturday night," Robin chimed in.

"Exactly. And that's where I think I'm stuck." Reagan walked back out of the closet again, her shoulders slumped down. "I feel like Jake has seen me in about every pair of shoes that I own at this point. So, I can't just say, 'Oh, I'll wear such and such heels because they're new,' you know?"

"But does it matter if he's seen them already? You all are hella together now, so I think he's going to see you repeat shoes every once in a while," I reminded her. In a way I understood what she was saying: she and Jake were just a few months into their reunited relationship, and, of course, she didn't want to risk it turning stale already. I knew all too well how easily that could happen. Still, five nights after my failed beer-tour date with Nick, Reagan had me equally chuckling and nervous at just how much pressure she was putting on herself and a pair of shoes.

I sat cross-legged on her bed as Reagan continued strutting around her shoe closet, trying on what felt like every shoe she owned as she picked out what she was going to wear when Jake visited from New York this weekend. We were all gathered for our regular nachos-and-margaritas catch-up, casually called Nacho Thursdays, even though it didn't always happen on Thursdays. This time, we were at Reagan's place in Columbia Heights.

It was always the four of us for these bimonthly meetups, at least since our friend Christine passed in April. Something about her death drew us even closer and solidified for each of us, without a word being said, the importance of making sure we continued our tradition. Each time, we'd meet at one of our apartments or one of our favorite Mexican restaurants in the city, and it didn't matter what else was going on, you could *not* miss this time. This was also in addition to whatever other times we met up for happy hours, brunches, promotions and tears (good and bad). We were *close.*

I'd known Reagan and Robin since college. Over time, we formed the original quartet with Christine, a booming, raspy-voiced, five-five Afro-Latina who didn't believe in living a life that avoided pain. She and Reagan—our charming, five-foot-three lover of shoes, solo dancing and perfectionism—had been friends since they were kids, both making the trip to DC from New Orleans to attend Howard University. There, they met me and Robin, a five-nine diva who maybe weighed 135 pounds at the time but had grown into her height and her confidence eight years later, proudly sporting her thick thighs and blond balayage lob while she slayed the corporate finance scene.

Rebecca joined our crew, briefly making it a quintet, when she and Reagan met at work and became inseparable. In the world of political journalism, Reagan had miraculously made friends with a reddish-blond-haired white woman with freckles like hers who had a tendency to laugh loud and long and get to work no later than 9:00 a.m.—also like her. This was when they would spend time telling each other stories about their lives and loves before anyone else came walking through the door, coffee in hand, struggling to make it in by ten thirty.

It wasn't long before those conversations between the two of them led to invites to happy hours, and before we knew it, our quartet had grown. Now I couldn't imagine my life without either of these women, a fact we'd all had to contemplate when Chrissy's complications from gall-bladder surgery turned dire and she grew sicker as years passed, developing gastroparesis and later blood infections with her feeding tubes. Her death rocked us all, forever freezing us in a time period now known as ACD— *after Christine's death*. That meant even when we were traveling together or laughing or simply drinking margaritas, her loss loomed over us in this unspoken, tragic way.

Tonight was no different. If I allowed myself the space, I could almost hear Chrissy's roaring laugh as she watched the scene play out in front of her. And she wouldn't have been wrong in doing so. There we were, three of us spread across Reagan's bedroom, drunkenly watching her bounce in and out of her closet, agonizing over something that her boyfriend most likely wouldn't even notice. Of course, Reagan would never believe that. Even tonight, she was nonchalantly wearing thigh-high black studded socks from Rihanna's Savage line while the rest of us had on what normal people called casual on a Thursday at the end of a workday—Robin had on ankle socks, I wore some striped knee-high socks and Rebecca rocked her bare feet.

"I know. I just—"

Rebecca interrupted her. "You're just clearly trying to plan everything to a tee when you're supposed to be letting some things go, remember?"

"Of course I remember. And even if I didn't, I've got my diary here to remind me." She picked up the journal that sat in her closet next to a set of six different-colored pens and waved it at us. "Between y'all and the stories in this thing, how could I forget? It's just…don't y'all remember that early-on feeling when you were nervous and excited about everything? That's how I am with Jake right now. I know it all doesn't need to be perfect, but I kinda want it to be."

"I get that. Completely," Robin said, leaning forward from her seated position on the floor. "I remember before the first date I went on with Eric, I must have tried on at least twenty outfits until I finally settled on one. And then an hour before he was supposed to pick me up, I changed again." Robin was caught up in the details of her story, but I was fighting hard not to chuckle at her casually calling one of the royals by his first name. I guess he'd been her boyfriend, so of course she would, but it never failed to jump-start my giggles. And I was not alone.

"Well, first off, you were going on a date with a whole prince, so that makes sense," Rebecca laughed. "But also, it was a first date. Of course you'd be anxious and trying on multiple outfits. This one over here is freaking out about shoes for a date with a man she's known since college who has probably seen her in *and* out of everything she owns."

"Wow, just read me like I'm not here."

"I'm just saying."

"Whatever. You're married, so maybe it's different for you. Jenn, help me out here. You and Nick have been together for a few years, but I'm sure you still worry about what you wear when you see him, right?"

"Actually, I was just thinking about this," I started, leaning back onto Reagan's headboard. "I don't think I do, but also we're probably not the best example to compare yourself to right now."

"Wait, why not?" Reagan asked, finally fully stepping her whole body out of the closet so that she stood right in front of me.

"Well, I don't know. I think about how our first date was this picture-perfect time at the Arboretum, right? Y'all know, we held hands and strolled through the different gardens of flowers, from azaleas to hollies to magnolias and everything in between. Now that date? I agonized over every. Single. Thing that I wore for it, from what earrings I'd wear to set off my pixie cut down to how I could pull off some cute but comfy shoes. And it was important for me to do that because I was so excited about this guy and really wanted to make a great impression. Now, though? We just went on a date last week, and I literally pulled out the first cute, summery thing I saw in my closet. And even then, it felt like a waste of a bomb-ass outfit."

"Okay, now wait, you told me it was a stupid brewery tour, but not all this," Robin said with concern in her voice.

"I know. I didn't want to alarm you guys. But honestly, I felt so much worse after that date than I did before we went on it. Nick was Nick after, of course, and sort of perfect. But it had me wondering if this is what I want going forward."

"Oh, no, what happened?" they asked in unison.

"Nothing, really, but that's kind of the point," I began. "We went on this date that any sane boyfriend would not have planned for a girlfriend who hates beer. Then we got back to his place, and he was asleep by 9:00 p.m. Like, what am I supposed to do with that?"

"Yeah, that's not great," sighed Robin. "So, there was no sexy time whatsoever?"

"Nope, not really. I mean he tried to be a little flirty, but ultimately, it didn't go anywhere. The thing is, though, I'm not even sure that my problem is just him." I braced myself to tell my friends a hard truth. "I've been feeling lately like I'm the boring friend, period. So maybe that energy is spilling over into my relationship. It's like, I spend so much time at my school, cleaning up, haranguing kids all around, and what else do I have going on in my life besides that and a boring relationship with my partner who only wants to sit around watching TV all night or goes to sleep by nine?"

"Wait, wait…you think you're boring? Since when? Why?" Reagan plopped down next to me on the bed and got comfortable as she peppered me with questions.

"Are you kidding me? You're the same person who up and quit her job last year, right, and then landed at her dream job just a few months later? And you…" I said, turning to Robin, "dated a freaking prince! Hello! And let's not forget you and Oliver, who are just the definition of whatever is the opposite of me and Nick. Fiery. Spicy. Passionate. All the things."

My last comment was directed to Rebecca, so she spoke up first in response to my mini tirade.

"Well, Olly and I have found what works for us, Jenn. But that didn't happen overnight. We've been married ten years. If you and Nick are invested in this relationship, you'll figure out the same. That doesn't mean it has to look like what Oliver and I have."

"True. You can find spice that isn't going to sex clubs two or three times a month." Robin winked, clearly trying to lighten the mood.

"Exactly. You might decide a swingers' club once

a week works better for you," Rebecca said in a dead-pan voice that inspired the laugh I needed right in the moment.

"Okay, okay, I get it. I'm not saying I want exactly what you all have. Just that I look at you, and I'm like, man, these girls are out here taking on the world. And honestly, it's hard for me to say this, but sometimes I just feel left behind. Like I have no story worth telling."

"Jenn, please don't feel that way," Reagan said, scooching closer to me so that she could put her hand on my knee. "First of all, there's no such thing as being left behind in this group. We might all be on different journeys at times, but we love each other too much for that to happen. Second, Rob and I have known you since college, and you've never really been the person who wants the chaos of our lives. So, if that's changed? You know, tell us now, and we can make that happen. We can just blow some mess up in your life and give you all the anarchy you could ever want," she laughed. "I guess what I'm saying is, sure, you're not quitting your job on a whim after a guy stands you up at a Mardi Gras ball, but that's probably a good thing."

"And…" Robin jumped in. "It's not like the thing with Eric went anywhere. It's fun in theory to date a prince, but we all see how hard Meghan has it with her royal family. That mess is not for the faint of heart and definitely doesn't inspire this Black woman to want to try the same thing. So, that shouldn't count as something to be like, 'oh, Rob dated a prince, I'm not doing anything with my life because, what, I didn't also date a prince'?"

"It's not that, exactly," I laughed, and then felt my eyes start to get wet. Pausing to stop myself from getting too emotional, I took another sip of my drink and then continued. "I think what you all see as chaos in your lives, I'm starting to see as passion. And I look at my life and don't see that…anywhere. So, no, I don't necessarily need to date a prince or quit my job or have an open relationship, but something is missing. A lot of something is missing."

"Okay, I get that. I do," Reagan said. "But if you remember, it was you who pulled my coattail last year and convinced me to really make a commitment to doing the things on my risk list. So, we're all joking here, but if you really feel like something's missing, you can't be a bigger advocate for me than for yourself. Let's talk about what you want to do about it."

"That's the thing. I don't know where to start, Rae. I'm just sad all the time now. I play it off well, but it's all I feel some days." I could feel the tears aching to come down. It was all I could do to stop them, so I finally briefly closed my eyes and let a few make their way out and down my face in hopes it would prevent more from flowing. It wasn't like I thought my friends would judge me for it, but I just didn't want to be the girl ugly crying over nachos and margaritas.

"Well," Robin interjected, "it was also you who gently called me out for talking about wanting to find a therapist for six months and not doing anything about it. Maybe that's a place to start? It's helped me a lot, especially after my breakup."

"You're right, I did do that. The difference with both of those examples was that they were things you two had committed to, but you weren't doing. I've casually thought about therapy, and I believe it's something everyone should do, but I'm just not sure I'm ready for it. I also tried talking to Nick, and he just seems oblivious. I don't know, maybe I need more sleep or something…and a new job."

"A new job always helps," Reagan said, raising her pointer finger in the air to show her agreement.

"And more sleep's not a bad option, either." Robin leaned in closer to me before finishing her statement, putting her right hand on my knee. "But if you need more, that's okay, too. Honestly. We love you too much and we're all far too close for you to be sitting around feeling like this for more than a day or so and not talking to us about it."

"Yeah, I hear you. And that's why I'm saying it now. But it's also pretty embarrassing to admit. Who wants to say out loud that they feel how I feel, especially in relation to their friends? No one, I promise you."

"That's fair, but we couldn't help until you just said something. And even if we can't do anything else, we can do the most important thing, which is just be here with you while you figure it all out." Rebecca stood up as she was talking, picking up her almost-empty glass along the way, and then raised it to the sky. "Us, and our trusty margaritas!"

"Ha-ha, yes, you can't go wrong with margs," I chuckled, wiping off the tearstains that had started to dry up.

"Speaking of margs, I think we need a re-up, ladies. Am I right?" Reagan asked.

"Definitely." I unfolded my legs to begin climbing off Reagan's bed. The rest of the girls followed suit, picking up their glasses and standing up so that we could head back to her kitchen where whatever was left in the pitcher was waiting for us.

Robin grabbed my waist and pulled me to her side as we walked to the kitchen, putting her head slightly on my arm. I knew it was her silent way of saying *I got you*, and I caught myself so that I wouldn't start crying again. Why had I taken so long to tell them how I was feeling? If nothing else, all three of these women had shown me over and over that we had each other's backs. I guess it's just always hard to admit when you're the one who needs help.

Breaking myself out of my thoughts, I turned the attention back to Reagan, right as we all entered the kitchen. She was in midpour.

"Don't think we forgot about you, though, Rae. What's going on with this meticulous shoe picking? Are you trying to overplan your weekends with

Jake so that they are perfect and then by default that means y'all are perfect?"

"Thank you!" Rebecca screamed and threw up her hands dramatically. "This is what I was trying to say earlier. It's giving me old Rae. This man loves you and you love him. Who cares what shoes you wear to dinner?"

"Okay, everything you just said was blasphemous to a person who curates shoe of the day posts on social media. Hi, have we met? You know I plan my whole outfit based on what shoes I'm wearing."

"Yes, yes, I know. But this feels…different."

"Ugh!" Reagan took a gulp of her drink before handing off the pitcher to Robin so that she could pour her own glass. "Maybe it is, I don't know. I don't know! How did this even come back to me? We were fully dealing with Jenn's problems."

"I'm pretty sure we can all walk and chew gum at the same time," Robin responded. "Yes, we're here for Jenn, but before we leave, we've got to make sure you have your last pair of shoes picked out, and then we need to make sure the next time Jake comes to town, you're not doing this again."

"Wait, you're still going to help me?"

"Of course. We're not sadists," Rebecca said, already walking back to the bedroom with a full glass. "Plus, we know if we left before you picked it out, you'd just be in the damn closet all night, agonizing over this decision. I'm just saying in the future, it may be time to reconsider why you're super invested in making sure you're wearing the perfect date shoes with this man."

"Okay, okay, that's fair. I promise I will consider." Reagan put her glass down on the coaster on her tan nightstand and gave Rebecca a big hug. "Thanks, Becs!"

"Yeah, yeah. Go run into that closet. You know that's where you want to be."

Reagan's smile grew as she shimmied her shoulders and danced her way back to her closet. Once inside, she called back out to us. "So, I think I have an idea."

We heard some rustling for a minute or so, something that sounded like a box or two falling, then a shuffle, and finally out popped Reagan holding a pair of lime-green heeled sandals that looked like they were meant to tie their way up a woman's calf. If my eyes were correct, they were at least four and a half, maybe five-inch stilettos with zero platform. "What about these babies?"

"It's for dinner, right? Where you're going to be sitting down most of the time?" I asked.

"Yep!"

"Then they're perfect."

"The perfect date shoes," Rebecca joked.

Chapter Three

By 11:30 p.m., we'd all had our fair share of margaritas and nachos, I'd cried in front of my friends, and Reagan had picked out which shoes she was going to wear when she saw Jake in a few days. I'd call that a fairly successful evening. It was just enough time for each of us to try to catch the Metro train from Columbia Heights before it shut down at midnight. But with Rebecca living in Northern Virginia and me in the Bloomingdale area of the city, the chances that we'd have time to make our transfers were slim. Robin lived much closer, in the Petworth neighborhood, but five-plus glasses of margaritas each didn't sound like the best mind-set for either of us trying to navigate the subway system late at night.

I leaned on Reagan's foyer wall as I scrolled through my phone to pull up my trusty Lyft app, while Becs and Robin did the same, making sure to compare prices to see whether Uber or Lyft made more sense for them. Within a few minutes, each of our cars were pulling up.

"Don't forget to let me know when y'all get home," Reagan said while giving out her final hugs of the evening.

"We won't forget," we said in unison.

"For Jennifer?" I asked, turning back to the driver of the car I'd requested.

"Yep. To Q Street, right?"

"Right. Thanks."

I climbed into the car and immediately settled back into the seat for my trip home.

"You don't mind if I just close my eyes for a bit, do you?"

"No, feel free. Just don't throw up."

"Don't worry. I'm more tired than drunk."

Taking in a deep breath, I thought of how good it felt to be open with my friends about how I'd been feeling lately. And the contrast of how lonely I'd felt lying next to Nick the other night. How had we gotten there, I wondered. It wasn't like Nick was a bad guy—far from it. But somewhere along the lines our relationship had lost the spark I adored. I shut my eyes, letting my mind wander back to those first few months when we'd just started dating and I quickly knew that he was the guy for me.

Our chemistry was undeniable then. Sexy, yes, but also filled with a tenderness I'd never experienced before him. And a starvation, too. We craved each other endlessly; just the thought of his fingers on my skin could have sent me into a deep, lasting orgasm. But it wasn't just about the sex. It was that I believed our sexual chemistry was rooted in a love for each other that even we couldn't explain early on, and it only grew as we continued our relationship. I would never have thought those two lovebirds would be in a rut where they hadn't been intimate in months, but we were. And for some reason, Nick—the guy who knew how to seduce every inch of my body—didn't seem to notice.

"What kind of wine did you bring again?"

It was a fall night in DC and Nick's and my fifth date, so I finally suggested that he come over so that I could cook dinner for us. I was in the kitchen sautéing shrimp, okra, sausage and cauliflower rice all in a huge pan—a twist on a recipe my grandma used to make for us when she was younger—while he aired out the wine. And Nick was in my dining room, opening the bottle of wine he brought with him.

"It's a Spanish rioja. I figured since you wouldn't tell me what you were cooking, I'd just bring a wine that I really like."

"Well, it worked out perfectly. I've never tried that before, so I'm looking forward to it."

"Oh, you haven't?" he asked, pouring my glass

with a devilish smirk on his face. "Well, you have to at least take one sip now so you can tell me what you think."

Nick walked toward me, wineglass in hand, and stood dangerously close to me as he tipped the glass toward my lips so that I could keep stirring as I sipped.

"Mmm," I moaned lightly as I let the smooth wine drip down my tongue. "Okay, that's really good."

"Yeah?"

He stepped even closer to me and put the glass on my kitchen counter.

"Let me taste."

Gently wrestling the cooking spoon out of my hand, he lifted my chin up so that our lips met each other's as if they were always meant to connect so seamlessly.

"Yeah, I think you're right. Pretty tasty."

My breathing sped up as I took in his scent and felt his body pressing up against mine ever so slightly. Before I even realized it, he'd positioned me in a corner of the kitchen where my back was against the wall, his right hand was on my hip and my knees were growing weaker with every moment.

Nick kissed me again, drawing me closer to him with that same right hand, now situated on the small of my back and applying a gentle pressure that signified with all certainty where I belonged. Too much more of this and I knew that I was going to be putty in his hands, but nothing in me wanted him to stop. I was too busy enjoying the mix of smooth and rough ridges that made up his lips and how they intertwined with mine, as well as the feel of his back and shoulders as my hands made their way up and down his spine.

"Wait," I said, finally gaining some composure. I cleared my throat before speaking again to make sure actual verbal words would come out of my throat. "If we don't stop, the food's going to burn."

"Mmm, that's a good point."

"Right?"

"Yeah, but there's something I can do to help that." In one fell swoop, Nick leaned his body toward the stove, turned it off and then focused his attention back onto me. Staring into my eyes with a desire that I'd only fantasized about experiencing, he spoke to me in a tone that was barely above a whisper.

"Thing is," he said, "that dinner smells sooo good, but the only thing I really want to eat tonight is you."

And with that, before I could say another word, he scooped me up and walked us to my bedroom, placing me on my bed as he continued kissing me. Chills crawled down my spine as I watched him undress, meticulously but quickly unbuttoning his shirt. His biceps tensed up when he peeled each sleeve off and then brought his body back over mine.

"Do you want this, Jennifer?"

"Yes."

I wasn't sure if sound came out when I spoke, so I

made sure to nod my head as well. There was nothing I wanted more than him right then.

"Good, because I've been thinking about licking you and making you come on my face since the day we met." He stared into my soul as he said each word. Somehow, it ensured that I couldn't take my eyes off him either, a fact that gave him all the power in the room.

With the consent he needed, he leaned back over me and grabbed the bottom of my tank top, swiftly sliding it up above my waist, then my shoulders, and over my head. With my red lace bra exposed to him and my chest lifting and falling as I took in each breath, he stopped just long enough to allow his eyes to pierce mine and then glide over my body. It was something about being watched by him that turned me on even more, and I think he knew it, so he reveled in it before slowly skimming his hands down the sides of my thighs. Nick paused when he got to the hem of my flowy skirt, lifted it up slightly so that he could get his hands underneath and grabbed the edges of my panties. With a slight pull, he slipped them under my butt and down my legs, leaving me completely open to him.

"Mmm," he moaned into my vagina and pressed his face into the folds between my legs, at first alternating between gentle bites on my lips and quick flicks of his tongue on my clit.

"Oh my God, you're such a tease."

He lifted his head up slightly.

"Nah, I just want you to crave me."

He hesitated for a bit and then gave me that same smirk from the kitchen before proceeding back to his position. This time, he softly blew on my clit and used his middle finger to trace small circles right on the tip, expertly maneuvering his finger almost like his tongue but in a way that he could admire his work as my juices began to trickle down.

"Niiiiick," I let out and took in a shallow breath.

"Yes?"

"Pleeeease."

"Please what?"

"Please stop torturing me!"

"But what do you want me to do?" He cricked his neck to the side as he awaited my response. Even as I pleaded with him, he hadn't stopped teasing me, now taking his middle finger and inserting it into me, finding just the right spot inside to send chills through me.

"Lick me. Suck my clit. I don't know, something! Pleaaaase. I just need it now."

"As you wish."

His mission accomplished, Nick bent his face back down and clenched his lips directly onto my clit. Sucking it like his life depended on it while also flicking his finger on my G-spot within. He kept the same pace for a while and then would switch up his stroke, going from flickers to full-on multifinger penetration, but not once did his mouth let go of my clit. That, he just kept sucking on and sucking on, until I felt my entire body tingle and tighten, and my hands grabbed the back of his head as I exploded all over his face, my sheets and my thighs.

"Wow. I've never... Wow!"

I tried catching my breath, but everything on me was suddenly super sensitive to touch, and I thought I'd been transported to this otherworldly dimension where orgasms start in your vagina and make their way throughout your entire body, down to your toes, into your eye sockets and all the way through the follicles of hair on your head. It wasn't like I'd never had an orgasm before, but this took over my whole being in a way that all my body could do was squirt out its excitement.

"Good. I like doing something for you that no one else has."

Nick slid back up my frame and lay down directly next to me, his skin colliding with mine in a way that felt really intimate, even more than what we'd just done, but somehow not in an invasive way. If he could have taped his limbs to mine at that point, I wouldn't have minded. He slung his right arm over my upper body, pulling me into him and turning me so that we now faced each other, our sweaty chests stuck together.

"Do you have other plans tonight? Because if you have a little more time, I can get up and finish cooking, if you want. Once I can stand on my legs again, of course," I whispered to him, sort of joking. The truth was I didn't want him to leave at all, but we'd only known each other less than a month, and I didn't want to assume that he was planning to spend the night, or even that he didn't have plans after our date. I was also a little worried about how wobbly my legs would be if I stood up too soon.

"Plans? Why would I want to go anywhere else? You trying to kick me out, Ms. Pritchett?"

"Definitely not. Just giving you an out if you want it, that's all."

"Ah, well, I'm at my happiest when I'm with you. So, I'm good right where I'm at."

Nick couldn't see my smile grow to the size of Texas as I burrowed my face into his collarbone, but he might have felt it. Those were the exact words a girl wanted to hear from the guy she felt herself starting to fall for. They were certainly music to my ears.

"Okay, then. Good. Me, too."

"And as for dinner, I'm full now. But maybe we can pick that back up in a bit, too."

Fully satisfied, I rested my head on his chest and fell fast asleep in his arms.

Seven minutes after I settled into my Lyft car, we pulled up to my apartment, the redbrick row house that held four apartments. One on the basement level, mine on the first floor—which required walking up a flight of black wrought iron steps before you got to it—and then two others on the second and third floors.

"Thanks! Have a good night," I called out to the

driver as I climbed out of his car and closed the door behind me. Making my way up the stairs, I walked inside the building and turned left to unlock the door that served as the entrance to just my apartment. It was cold and dark when I stepped inside, which was a stark reminder that I'd forgotten to turn the air off when I'd left earlier that day. At my door, I flicked off my nude slip-on sneakers with the kind of relief you can only get from finally being home. Without turning on the lights, I walked past my living room, dining room and kitchen, and immediately went to my bedroom, which faced the back of the house.

In the dark, I found a long T-shirt from my dresser and quickly changed into it, removing my shirt, shorts and bra with ease. I grabbed my satin scarf from my nightstand and practically tied it around my head with my eyes closed. The only thing I wanted after such a long day was to feel the comfort of my sheets and my duvet cover insulating me in bed. Closing my eyes somehow made it feel like it was already in progress. Finally, I climbed into my bed and pulled the covers over me almost like a tent, ready to isolate myself from the immense sadness I felt after remembering what Nick and I used to have.

A light from my phone reminded me that I hadn't told anyone I'd made it home yet.

Reagan: Y'all home yet?

Robin: I am. Got home a couple minutes ago. Sorry, was just about to say so.

Reagan: No worries. All good.

I am, too, I texted back, jumping in before any-one could worry.

Reagan: Okay, great.

Rebecca: Almost. I should be home in another ten.

Reagan: Awesome. Let us know, Becs.

Rebecca: Will do.

With that settled and knowing almost everyone was back home safely, I silenced my phone, placed it on my nightstand and made sure to turn it over so that I wouldn't be disturbed by the light going off when Rebecca texted again. Sure, I wanted to see that she got home, too, but most importantly, I needed uninterrupted quiet time. Sliding back into my duvet cocoon, I closed my eyes tightly, wishing it was that easy to shut off all my thoughts as well.

Chapter Four

Cynthia is a middle child with an older and younger brother. She loves Barbies.

Kevin wants to be the Black Panther.

Lucy taps her pencil on her desk when she's nervous.

The following Monday morning, I was back in my classroom, reading off reminders I'd left on various sticky notes on my desk to help me remember something personal about each kid. In a month, I wouldn't need the Post-its anymore, but I'd learned it could be tricky to try to remember everything all at once at the start of a new school year. These were my saving grace until I'd developed a close enough relationship with each student where I no longer needed them.

When I first started out as a teaching assistant at Kendall Elementary—DC's premier public charter grade school—I'd perpetually beaten myself up for remembering a kid's name but not their story or vice versa. I could usually play it off, because kids under ten are so beautifully innocent and generally want to believe whatever adults tell them, but inside, I was melting down about being such a disappointment. It took just one time to scare me enough that I knew I had to come up with some kind of mind trick to help myself.

It was my first year as the lead teacher, about three years later, and a student came running back into my classroom because he'd forgotten his toy car in his cubby. As soon as I saw his adorable little chubby face, his name drained out from the recesses of my brain. It was only his second day at school, and there he was, unwittingly staring down his teacher who couldn't have recalled his name if it meant I'd win a multimillion-dollar lottery. Instead, I just littered him with "sweethearts" and "honeys," told him everything was okay, and watched him retrieve his toy from the cubby that had the sticker with his name on it. My heart sank when I saw the name associated with the cubby he went toward. Damien. His name was Damien. And I was a horrible teacher. I knew right then I'd never be put in that position again.

Caresha wears a cheerleader pom-pom pendant on her book bag from her older sister.

Jared scrunches his nose when he's thinking of an answer.

By the time I read through the seventeen notes four times each, I felt confident enough to get through the morning. I looked up at the clock that I'd hammered into my back wall about a month earlier when I was decorating my classroom with HBCU memorabilia, photos of my favorite Black artists and entertainers across the diaspora, and quotes from other youngish people whom my students could look up to like Malala Yousafzai, Greta Thunberg and X González. I had fifteen minutes left to prepare myself before a flurry of kids would come running into my classroom with backpacks almost as big as they were. Just enough time to get in some mindless scrolling on Instagram while drinking my coffee and taking in the last quiet moments I'd have again until about 3:00 p.m.

I pulled my phone out of the side drawer that I kept it in, on silent, during the day and quickly realized that I wasn't about to have the peaceful scrolling experience I'd just pictured. Somehow, in the forty minutes since I'd been at work, I'd missed thirty-six texts and counting. Before I could panic and think someone had died, I unlocked my phone and saw that it was the text chain with my girls blowing up.

Reagan: I just don't know how this could have happened!!

Robin: Rae, we're so sorry. So sorry.

Reagan: What am I going to do?!

Clearly something had gone horribly wrong. I texted a reply letting them know I was now in the conversation, too.

Hey, everyone, sorry, I had my phone in my desk. Catching up now.

It's okay, Jenn. We figured, replied Robin in a split second.

Doom scrolling my way back up to when the messages started, I finally came across the one that kicked it off—a text from Reagan that none of us wanted to see.

Jake and I broke up this weekend. It's over for good this time.

Quickly scanning through, I learned that they'd gotten into a huge argument when he came to town over the weekend. Apparently, Jake admitted that the long distance was weighing on him but wouldn't go as far as asking her to move to New York so that they could be together. Rae was hurt by the assumption that she would be the one to move and that long distance was once again an issue for them, as if they didn't know where they each lived when they decided to try dating again. In true Reagan fashion, she blamed the fight on the fact that, at the last minute, she'd scratched her usual routine of planning out their weekend—and her shoes that went with it. This was what leaving things to chance looked like to her. Thank God she wasn't also blaming us for pushing her to do so.

After sufficiently catching myself up, I texted them back.

Rae, oh my God. I'm so sorry. I don't even know what to say.

Reagan: Thanks, Jenn.

There really is nothing to say.

I'm just done.

I should have known better.

In just four back-to-back texts, she'd broken my heart. If there was one thing I knew, it was that we were all meeting up tonight to be with her through this pain. I had plans with Nick, but not until much later, and I figured he would understand if I was a little late; this was DEFCON-level bad. Unfortunately, I'd also eaten up all my time catching up on the older texts, and I could hear the familiar loud sounds of children in the hallway.

I have to go, babes, the kids are coming in. But count me in for any plans tonight. You already know I'm there!

I slipped my phone back into my side drawer just as the first student came bouncing into my class, her cheerleader pom-pom pendant swinging from her backpack.

"Good morning, Caresha! So good to see you today."

"Hi, Miss Jenn!"

"Did you enjoy your weekend?"

"OMG. Yes. My sister? She showed me how to do front flips yesterday."

"Wow! That's so exciting."

"Oh, yes. I'm really good, Miss Jenn."

"I bet you are, sweetheart."

Caresha's smile was as wide as the ocean as she detailed her weekend. She was so happy telling her story that she stopped in the middle of the walk to her desk to nod her head to me once more, in case I needed more convincing that she, in fact, was really good. All I could do was laugh. *Note to self: add that confidence to her Post-it note.*

Within a minute, the rest of the students were piling into my classroom. with echoes of "Hi, Miss Jenn" filling in the air. This was the part I loved about being a teacher—seeing their eager faces at the start of the day, watching them take in the world around them and knowing that they were all sponges ready to soak up whatever I gave them. It was the exhaustion I felt at the end of the week and thoughts of not using the degrees my parents paid for that held me back from completely loving it, though.

"All right, babes, if you can hear me, clap three times."

Clap. Clap. Clap.

"Does that mean it's time for us to be in our chairs?" a small voice asked from the back of the classroom. He had on a Black Panther T-shirt.

"That's a great question, Kevin. It normally just means I want to make sure that you're listening to me. But right now, yes, it means I want to tell you all to have a seat so that we can get our morning started."

"I knew it." He was so proud of himself.

"Very impressive," I said, giving him a wink of validation.

The pitter-patter of their feet took up the air in the room as they all made their ways to their seats, expending the most energy ever to walk less than ten feet. This was combined with the sounds of chairs scratching the surface of the floor and restrained giggles, but in less than two minutes, they were all seated, looking up at me and waiting for their next direction.

"All right, babes, I am very excited for this morning's lesson. Do you know why?"

"Noooooo," they responded in unison.

"Well, today, one of you will get to point to something on my all-time favorite globe," I said, directing their attention to the twelve-inch structure that sat on a gold base. "And all week, we're going to learn everything we can about the food that the people who live there eat, the languages they speak and many of their traditions. So, who wants to pick?"

Seventeen arms flew up instantly, but one little amber-colored arm was shaking as she waved furiously. "Cynthia! Looks like you want to be a travel agent today."

"Mmm-hmm, yes, Miss Jenn. Please."

"Are you ready for this responsibility?"

Crinkling her nose like Jared as she considered my question, Cynthia took a beat before she answered. I could see her really wondering to herself, *Am I ready? Can I do this?* I hoped she knew the answer was an emphatic yes, but even if she didn't, she'd know by the time she graduated from my class. Along with teaching my kids the basics of math, science, reading and social studies, I saw it as my duty to make sure they each stepped into fourth grade fully assured of themselves and confident in their abilities…well, as much as one could be at eight or nine years old.

"I'm so ready," she said with a twinkle in her eye.

"Perfect. I knew you were anyway. All right, now come up here, because we have to get to the most important part before you point to the globe."

"What's that?" she asked.

"Well, first, you have to twirl around for fifteen

seconds. Then, I will swipe the globe so that it starts spinning, and you get to make it stop by putting your finger on it. Wherever your finger lands, that's what we're studying this week."

"What if it lands in an ocean?"

"I guess that means we'll be learning about the ocean, then."

Her eyes widened, and I could tell that was absolutely not what she wanted to have happen.

"Okay, class, are you going to help me count Cynthia's fifteen seconds?" I asked, turning my body so that I faced the rest of the students.

"Yessss!" they all shouted back.

Pleased with their response, I bent down next to Cynthia and whispered so that only she could hear me. "You got this," I said and then stood back up so that I could give out my last set of directions before we started.

"Okay, Cynthia, when we start counting, you start twirling. On the count of three. One, two, three…"

"One Mississippi, two Mississippi, three Mississippi, four Mississippi…" the class began counting with me, and Cynthia dutifully started her twirl. Her blue dress almost looked like it propelled around and around as her black leather T-bar shoes kept her from falling. In that moment, I noticed we both had on black leather shoes. Mine just happened to be pointed-toe flats from ASOS with huge black bows on the top, but they were more alike than they were different. Fifteen seconds later, Cynthia was done twirling and ready to make her pick.

As promised, I gently swung the globe to get it started moving on its axis, and she wasted no time placing her finger on it so that it would stop moving. This time, my smile widened when I saw where she landed. Bending down once again, I spoke to her first so that she knew she'd done a great job before I addressed the rest of the students.

"Amazing pick, Cynthia. I couldn't have done it better.

"Class, let's thank Cynthia for being such a great travel agent this morning!"

"Thank youuuuu, Cynthia!"

She walked back to her desk with an extra skip in her step, beaming from her recent accomplishment.

"So, this week—" I paused to make sure that they were as excited as I was. "We're going to be learning all about Benin."

By the time my planning period rolled around, I was eager to see what I'd missed in the text chain. I was sure that there would be a litany of plans made that I could just jump right into. Plopping down in my chair, I briefly took in the smells from my lunch— leftover barbecued ribs, macaroni and cheese, and green beans—before reaching back into my trusty drawer to grab my phone. *Mmm.* If there was one thing that I really enjoyed about being an adult, it was having the freedom to do practically whatever

I wanted as long as it didn't hurt anyone else. Today, that meant relishing in some soul food on a Monday afternoon while my students ate Lunchables and fruit snacks and had recess outside my four walls. With a rib in one hand, I unlocked my phone with the other.

Just as I suspected. Sixty-four missed texts. My friends were nothing if not consistently verbose. I scrolled through, making my way back to the last text I sent so that I could understand what was happening this time before chiming in.

Do you think when you all calm down, you can fix it? Rebecca had asked almost immediately after I'd put my phone away. I just don't see this being the end. Not after all the pride and fear BS that you both had to overcome to find your way back.

Reagan: That's the thing, Becs. We were both beaucoup calm by the end. It was like this awful feeling of inevitability. We knew better.

Scroll, scroll, scroll.

Robin: But he loves you. I know he does.

Reagan: I know he does, too…now. But maybe love just isn't enough.

Scroll, scroll, scroll.

Reagan: I just need to move on. Find someone new to get over the one who flew, you know?

Rebecca: That's not exactly how that saying goes.

Reagan: Whatever. You know what I mean.

Robin: Of course we do. And if that's how you really feel, we will support you. You can always do a date pact with me.

Reagan: Wait, tell me more about this.

Robin: Okay, so I had a coworker do this with some of her friends before, and they really enjoyed it. Basically, we promise to go on at least one date a week for a set amount of time. No excuses.

Reagan: Bet. Let's do it.

Wait, what? I stared at my phone in disbelief. Here I'd thought I was missing plans to bring ice cream and champagne to our sister's apartment this evening, but apparently what I'd really missed were Robin and Reagan making date-pact plans? I kept scrolling to see if somehow Rebecca had talked them out of it.

Rae, are you sure you want to jump into a dating pact the day after you broke up with the love of your life? Becs asked. I knew it. I could always count on Rebecca to try to curtail the mess when I wasn't there.

Reagan: I couldn't think of a better time to do it, honestly.

Rebecca: Okay.

Or not, I guess. Clearly, Becs had decided not to fight Rob and Rae on this idea, but everyone knew what that lonely "Okay" meant. She didn't approve, and I wasn't totally sure I did, either, to tell the truth. Reagan liked to think she was numb to feelings, but she was a big softy like me.

Reagan: This will be great. I really need to move on from Jake once and for all.

Robin: I'm looking forward to it! And honestly, I'm so ready to have someone in my life other than you three and my family who I can celebrate my accomplishments with. No shade to y'all, of course.

Rebecca: No, we get it. I'm incredibly thankful for Olly, so if this helps you two...then who am I to crap on it?

A familiar pang hit my chest as I continued scrolling and reading about their plans. Part of me started to like the idea, especially when I read that Reagan had been in bed all day. Maybe it was the jolt that she and Robin needed. So, was it that I didn't approve, or was I jealous that Robin and Reagan were almost guaranteed to have some more wild stories come out of this pact, and I'd be relegated to the boring one once again? I wondered.

Rebecca: So, wait, do you want us to come by tonight? You know we'll be there in a heartbeat if you need us.

Reagan: I know. But I think I need to be alone tonight. Rob, can we talk more about the pact tomorrow? My eyes hurt just as much as my heart now, so I think I need to go back to bed.

Robin: Of course, doll.

That's where the conversation had ended almost an hour before my planning period. It didn't seem like there was much left for me to contribute, so I shot off an obligatory Can't wait to hear more about this pact and resumed eating my lunch. I had about thirty more minutes to enjoy the peace and quiet, plot out my ideas for the rest of the week now that I knew what country we were closely examining, and maybe even figure out how to seduce my boyfriend, especially since there was no need to change my plans for the evening.

Chapter Five

"Byeee, Miss Jenn."

By 3:00 p.m., the students were packing their book bags at their desks and racing out of my class like they all had jobs to get to when they left.

"Au revoir, babes!" I called behind them. "Don't forget, tomorrow we say 'bonjour' or 'kudo' when we arrive, right? Does anyone remember why?"

A little arm flew up, her pencil tapping steadily in the air since she was no longer sitting at her desk.

"Yes, Lucy?"

"Because those are two ways to say 'hello' in Benin."

"Yes, that's right. And do you remember what languages those are?"

"French and, um…" She paused for a second, and I could see the way she was trying to remember our lesson all over her face. "Fon?"

"Yes, Lucy. That's absolutely correct. Good job!"

"I knew it," she whispered and pumped her fist in the air.

"You did that," Cynthia said to her and then gave her a high five.

What a perfect way for the school day to end. I watched them all as they went out, waiting for the last one to leave before I began my daily routine of putting the room back together. I liked walking into a classroom that looked brand-new in the morning, and I suspected, somewhere deep down in their little souls, the students liked it, too. One by one, I went to each desk and scooched the chair back in, wiped down the area with Clorox wipes, and inspected for random remnants of gum that seemed to pop up occasionally. In the right corner of the room, I picked up the papers that were strewn everywhere from today's English assignment, taking each one and placing it in the respective kid's assignment mailbox. Thankfully, the students had already done a great job of putting the math link cubes and number tiles back into their containers, so the math corner didn't take long for me to straighten up. But the arts section was a disaster. With a deep sigh, I dutifully rearranged all the art supplies back into their respective bins—dry-erase markers, pushpin whiteboard magnets, colored paper, pencils, highlighters, glue sticks, flash cards, glitter containers and more.

When the clock struck 4:00 p.m., I was officially wiped out and ready to be magically transported into the arms of my boyfriend. Unfortunately, the government or Big Tech hadn't quite figured out how to do that yet (speaking of, weren't we supposed to have Jetsons mobiles by now?), so I still needed to make my way across town by Metro, pick up dinner for me and Nick, and walk the last few blocks to his apartment. It wasn't a horrible commute; I'd probably be at his apartment in the next hour at most. But it certainly wasn't the same as wishing I was in his arms and then *boop*, I'm there!

I just had one last thing to do before I left: call Italian Kitchen on U and place our order to go. With any luck, the food would be ready when I got there and I could shave off another fifteen minutes before I walked through Nick's front door. The ever-present question these days was when would he get there?

"Mmm, Jenn, it smells so good in here."

The sun was starting to set when Nick finally got home about three hours after me. In that time, I'd worked on some more plans for the week, researching all that I could about Benin's traditions and culture and going over creative ways to review some of the math equations that caused a few of the students trouble. I'd also done some yoga and Pilates to release tension in my muscles and try to keep my size-six frame despite the barbecue I ate for lunch and the Italian we were going to eat tonight. And I worked out the perfect plan to introduce some spice back into Nick's and my relationship, starting with how I'd greet him when he walked in.

I didn't expect it to be a panacea to our problems. After all, more than a week had already gone by and Nick's promise to make up for the brewery tour had yet to materialize. In fact, since then, things had gone right back to the same routine—one of us at the other's apartment, eating, watching TV and going to sleep. But while my plans for tonight were also homebound, I had hopes for a vastly different outcome.

"I decided to pick up food from Italian Kitchen," I responded to him from upstairs. "I know how much you love their food."

"Ooh, yes, I do."

Even without seeing him, I knew that Nick's focus was most likely purely on the food in front of him—lasagna, baked feta and marinara on toasted wedges of bread, and caprese salad. If I knew my boyfriend, and I did, his mouth was watering, and he was struggling not to dig in before I joined him, which was going to ultimately make my meticulously planned entrance into the living room that much more shocking and sweet.

"I'll be down in just a second, but feel free to dig in without me," I said, continuing my plan to throw him off my scent.

"Nah, it's cool. I might get a little toasted wedge after I wash my hands, but I'm good to wait."

From upstairs, I heard him drop his bag by the front door, slide off his shoes and walk to his kitchen. The water ran for exactly twenty seconds, as if he had a timer in his head, then the trash can top flipped open and closed, and I knew he'd dried his hands off with a paper towel and thrown it away. A few seconds later, I heard his familiar sigh as he sat on the couch, finally able to relax in his home. That was my cue.

Walking carefully down his steps so that I didn't trip, I gingerly put one bare leg in front of the other and held on to the railing for dear life. I'd walked up and down these steps for years, but I didn't want this to be the moment they betrayed me. When I'd walked about halfway down, I cleared my throat so Nick would look toward me.

Dutifully, he did. With a toasted wedge still in his mouth, I saw Nick lose his breath for a second, letting the food fully drop and land in his hand. *Just the reaction I was hoping for.* I kept walking, pointing my toes as I stepped down to make sure that my slender thighs flexed a bit as he stared at me. The silence between us was palpable. Neither of us spoke a word—neither of us dared to—until I was standing directly in front of him, my eyes poring over him with desire. I allowed him to take me all in— deeply moisturized chocolate-brown skin covered in only a teal lace bra and thong set and bronzer to highlight my cheeks.

"H-how am I supposed to want all this food you bought when all I want to devour now is the person standing in front of me?"

"Well, in the past, it was a pretty easy decision for you. Is it still?"

I looked at him longingly, praying that the answer was an emphatic yes.

"Hell, yeah."

Before he could finish his response, Nick pulled me down onto him by my waist and enveloped my lips with his. As he kissed me, the fingers of his right hand instinctively went to my hair, and the other hand positioned me so that I was straddling his legs to make our midsections connect. He released my lips just slightly as he grabbed my hair to pull my neck back, giving him the room to slide his tongue down my chin and over my neck and collarbone. Once there, he alternated between small bites and flicks of his tongue, sending chills directly down my spine, and waves of sensation to my brain and vagina. He was definitely ready to consume me, and I was all too willing to volunteer as tribute.

Satisfied with my position on him now, Nick's hands turned to their task of taking off my clothes. Slowly, he dragged one strap from my shoulder, down my back, until he reached the clasps on my bra, opening them with the flick of an expert wrist and exposing my now fully goose-bumped skin to the chilled air. His other hand dutifully helped slide my other strap down my arm as I focused my attention on getting his lips back onto mine. Our tongues were dancing inside the other's mouth, our breaths getting deeper and deeper, when I felt my nipples harden and my breasts completely become revealed to him.

He felt it, too. With a deep growl, he removed his lips from mine, stared into my soul for ten seconds and then buried his face into my chest. Under Nick's spell, my body was no longer my own. He bit and licked and twisted my nipples, making sure that if his mouth was on one breast, his hand was on the other, and I could barely think beyond however he was manipulating my form in the moment. All I knew was that whatever he was doing had me dripping past the thin fabric of my thong onto his pants, which had a very distinct, hard member aching to get out.

In another swift move, Nick repositioned us on the couch so that my back was now on the seat cushions, my legs were on his shoulders and he was perfectly placed to be able to slide off my underwear without resistance. Even with this inherent power over me, Nick took his time, slowly dragging the sides of the thong down my hips, past my butt, around my thighs and over my feet until I was completely naked on the couch. I felt his eyes look me up and down, starting at my face and traveling down my exposed figure, inch by inch. He was hungry for me, and I was desperate for him.

Just then, I heard another growl come from him. But this time it wasn't a sexual rumble—it was one of actual hunger, coming from his stomach instead of his throat. As much as I wanted to, I couldn't not hear it.

"Wait, are you…are you actually hungry?" I asked, putting my hand on his head to gently stop him from doing anything else.

"I—" He paused but also released my legs from his shoulders so that he could fully sit up. "Kinda, yeah. I'm sorry."

I could see the sad expression on his face. It would be cruel for me to ignore that, but also, I was now lying naked on his couch and fully unprotected from the chilly air and my insecurities. I sat up as well, covering my breasts with my hands.

"Why didn't you say something?"

"I mean, you were standing there looking…how you looked. How could I? What kind of man—"

"What?" I asked, interrupting him.

He paused, the weight of what he was about to say blasting on his face.

"What kind of man chooses a plate of food over his girl?"

"An actual hungry one."

"Yeah, I guess so."

"Did you eat today?" I knew he'd been working more hours lately, so it occurred to me that maybe he'd lost track of time during the day and that's why he was so excited to come home to warm food. And instead, he'd walked into a trap set by his girlfriend who wanted him to prove he still desired her. Ugh.

"Nah, things got a little wild today. I had a green smoothie this morning, but that was it."

"Okay, so maybe let's take a pause and eat, then. Okay?"

"Are you sure you're okay with that?"

"Yeah, yeah, it's fine," I said, trying to convince myself as much as him. "Just…can I get your shirt to put on or something?"

"Oh, damn, yeah. I'm sorry."

Nick quickly tore through the buttons on his shirt, somehow swiftly releasing them without damaging any of them. Then he pulled me close to him so that he could help me put his shirt on. It was a small respite to the lump I felt building in my chest, but it didn't magically remove the questions soaring in my head. *Was I such an awful girlfriend that Nick felt he had to choose me over the lasagna or there would be consequences, even as he knew his body needed it? What did that say about us?* And this was now the second time in a little over a week when we'd started having sex and didn't. Five months ago, that was impossible. What did that say about us, too?

"I'm sorry, babe. I guess I was just really looking forward to eating, catching up on some of our shows together and relaxing tonight."

Nick's brown puppy-dog eyes could help him conquer the world. They certainly managed to help get him out of various sticky situations over the past

thirty years. And tonight, they were magically con-
trolling my brain so that the tight grip I had my fists
in from the stress building in my body began loos-
ening almost instinctively. I couldn't be mad at him,
of course. But I was sad for me. He'd all but just said
that our pause from sexy time wasn't really a pause
at all, but a stop for the evening. Once again, we'd
be up watching TV on the couch until I would inevitably hear his light snores, signaling the TV was
watching him more than vice versa.

In this moment, however, I knew he needed reas-
surance as much as I did. I placed my hand gently on
his cheek and mouthed, "It's okay, really."

A few tears threatened to fall from my eyes, but
I swallowed them and my doubts back down and
reached for my plate on the coffee table.

"I hope the food's still warm," I said, grabbing
the lasagna container so that I could scoop some
out onto my dish.

Nick had a mouth full of baked feta already, chewing it with delight.

"Honestly, babe, I'd eat it ice-cold right now. But
I think it's good to go."

Because he was still chewing, he sounded more
like the adults in *Charlie Brown*, but somehow, I still
understood him. It was the most adorable and frustrating thing he could have done, but that was Nick—
always making it super hard to hate him.

I added some of the caprese salad to my plate,
said a quick prayer and then started eating beside

him. The silence was unmistakable again, but not like before. This time, it was like the hush that falls over a dinner table when the food finally comes to a group of friends. Somehow, they all know that all other conversation that was taking place before the food arrived can be paused until they have a second to indulge their appetites. That was me and Nick now on his couch, mixed with a little bit of awkwardness and sexual frustration.

"How was your day?" I asked, finally daring to break the quiet. "You said it was hectic, right? What happened?"

"Sigh. We just had a lot of clients asking questions all at the same time, honestly."

"And the golden-boy accountant had to answer them all, of course?"

"That's why they pay me the big bucks, babe." He shrugged his shoulders and reached for another baked feta wedge to stuff into his mouth. "What about you? How was class?"

"No, I'm not letting you get out of that so easy. I know you've been working a lot lately, and I see the toll it's having on you. I just want you know that you can talk to me about it. Like maybe that might help us, too, you know."

"I know, I know. But, honestly, it's more stressful for me to dwell on it. So, I'd just rather not. You get it, right?"

Sadly, I did. A lot of Black men I'd grown up with had this same mentality where they didn't feel like they could—or maybe hadn't learned how to—talk about their feelings or express their frustrations. And while Nick was a fairly progressive, emotionally in-tune guy, his empathy was usually reserved for the people he loved. Not himself. I saw it anytime one of his brothers called and needed his attention im-mediately; he'd drop everything he was doing for them to just be a listening ear from across the coun-try. Or when he'd talk to me about wanting to make enough money to pay off his parents' mortgage be-cause he knew how much they'd sacrificed to get him and his brothers to where they were now—all college educated, some married with families, out in the world, blazing their own paths. I especially saw it when it came to me. Nick was always perfectly gentle with me; we were that couple that intertwined our fingers together whenever we walked, and he was never shy about spoiling me with forehead kisses and tight squeezes around my torso and encourag-ing me to love me.

But try to get him to admit that he was over-worked, and Nick would shut down almost instantly. So, whenever he said, "I'd rather not," I learned to leave it alone. Not just from my experience with him, but also from watching my mom and dad. Early on, I observed that when a man said he didn't want to talk about something, it was no use in trying to force him to do so. I saw my mom find other ways to get my dad to relax when she knew he was overworked—maybe the reason for a lot of the trips they took—

but she never pried. Still, something in me wanted to shake him and just plead with him to open up to me about this kind of stuff.

"Now, tell me about class, please," Nick said while continuing to stuff his face. He'd turned his body fully to me by that point to make sure that he showed he was listening to me even as he ate.

"Oh, right. Well, one of the kids ended up picking Benin as our country for this week, so I want to see if I can get permission for us to cook a Beninese meal at the end of the week. I'm thinking àkàrà, fufu, oranges, pineapples, and rice and beans."

"Damn! See? I wish you were my teacher in third grade. I would have paid way more attention."

"Ha! Well, let's see if I get permission first."

"You will. I already know it. Phillip and everyone at Kendall love you, so they're not going to tell you no. Not my baby!"

Nick winked at me like I wink at my kids when I want them to know they can do something. Maybe I'd gotten that from him over the years and hadn't realized it until now. Either way, it was definitely what I needed. Especially since I wasn't as confident as he was that Phillip, my vice principal, was going to say yes to such a big, out-the-box request.

"So, what do you say? Are we catching up on the Mayans tonight or *Snowfall*?" he asked, already picking up the remote control.

"I vote for *Snowfall*. I need to see what Franklin

has gotten into now. Plus, we're like three episodes behind, and I need my Damson Idris fix."

Nick snapped his head toward me again, somewhat jokingly, but kind of not. "All right, no Damson ogling tonight, please. Especially when your handsome boyfriend looks nothing like him."

"Yes, but my handsome boyfriend picked lasagna over me tonight, so I don't think he gets to say what ogling does and doesn't happen," I responded, playfully pushing him so that he knew I wasn't trying to be harsh.

"Oh, the dagger…in my chest…someone help take it out."

"Okay, okay. Enough." I rolled my eyes and sat back into the corner of the couch, placing myself in our usual position for TV watching.

Nick clicked the TV to our shared Hulu account, pressed Play on the episode and jumped up to turn the lights off. When he returned, he took another bite of lasagna and then sprawled his body over my lap just as the opening scenes began. I placed a bet in my head for how long it would be before I heard his familiar deep breaths and soft snores. An hour, tops, I figured. And then, like clockwork, I'd tell him to go to bed, clean up the living room and eventually join him upstairs. Same routine as always. Loving as hell, but absolutely no spark.

Chapter Six

Almost two weeks later, I found myself in another familiar position—frantically trying to leave work on a Friday afternoon so that I wouldn't be late meeting my friends for happy hour. My trusty wall clock stared me down, steadily reminding me that it was 5:30 p.m., then 5:45 p.m., then six. But from the looks of my classroom, I had at least another ten to fifteen minutes of cleaning to do before I could leave, which was definitely a problem, since we'd all agreed to meet at Stan's Restaurant by six.

And really, that was late for Stan's, the cocktail lounge tucked off to the side of Thomas Circle that served some of the best fried catfish in the city—and the strongest drinks. Over the years, Stan's had become a staple for Black DC, and it was known for many things—the way they gave you a tall glass of your liquor of choice and separate, smaller glass of chaser when you ordered things like whiskey and lemonade; that you could run into everyone from Howard alums you hadn't seen in years to future council members; and, most importantly, for my current situation, the fact that they did not take reservations on Friday nights. In fact, most DC natives and upwardly mobile Black folk in the city knew that if you got to Stan's after 6:00 p.m. on a Friday, the only thing you were guaranteed was standing around waiting for a table to eventually open up. I was screwed. And my friends were not going to be happy.

I got my first text at 6:05 p.m.

Reagan: Jenn, are you still at school? You can tell us the truth. We won't kill you.

The next one came in less than thirty seconds later from Robin.

Speak for yourself, Rae...

Reagan: They have a table ready for us, Jenn. But you know they won't seat us if everyone's not here.

I could see who was playing good cop and bad cop this time.

Maybe we can pretend she's here but like in the bathroom or something? proposed Rebecca.

Robin: Yeah, I'm fairly sure a million people have tried that trick before.

Reagan: Well, let's just see what we can do...more soon, Jenn. Don't ignore us, though!

With each text, my anxiety grew stronger. I knew there was no way I'd be able to magically appear behind them at the door in the next few seconds. But what could I say, really? *"Sorry, I know I said that I'd be there by 6:00 p.m., but you see, at 3:00 p.m., I had one student throw a full-on tantrum in the middle of class right as they were all packing their bags to leave. This meant that I had to keep him with me until all the other students were safely on their respective school buses, in line waiting for carpool or connected to a crossing guard so that they could walk home. And then I had to call his parents and explain that Derrick couldn't properly express that he wasn't ready for class to end, so he started throwing paint from our latest art project at the walls. And now I need to clean said walls."*

Sure, they'd understand, but not really.

I braced myself and began typing.

Rebecca: WAIT, we got seated!

Robin: Jenny, you better get here soon. A miracle of all miracles just happened, and we've basically put a purse and a jacket on the seat that is allegedly taken by YOU.

Oh, thank God, I thought. A Stan's miracle was just what I needed. Finally, I responded.

I promise I'll be there before your drinks get to the table. I'm finishing up the last thing now, calling a car and freshening up in the back seat.

I'm sure my Uber driver won't mind!

Order me a tequila soda pleaaaase.

With three back-to-back texts, I laid out my plans and hurriedly finished cleaning my classroom, tying up the final trash bag to throw out.

Robin: Okay, okay. Just get here soon.

Reagan: But like, maybe don't flash the Uber driver?

Rebecca: Well, they might like it. You never know.

Leave it to Becs to provide some levity.

Okay, I have to stop texting back so I can get there. See you soon!

* * *

Walking into Stan's can sometimes feel like walking into the *Cheers* bar—not because someone is going to scream out your name, though that could very well happen, but simply because it feels like the kind of cozy, secret spot that invites you and your friends to enjoy time with each other without all the flashiness and pretense that can come with a lot of DC lounges. If *secret* meant you and a couple other hundred people who were in on the underground experience, of course. The entire restaurant is at basement level, so the trek into it first requires traversing down the stairs, climbing your way through the crowd gathered at the front bar waiting to be seated and then emerging into a dimly lit oasis.

And I had to do all this in the heeled python-and-tan Alexandre Birman sandals that I'd slipped on in my Uber car on the way here. I threw them, fierce and backless, in my bag this morning, knowing I'd need to wipe the teacher smell off me come happy-hour time. But I'd forgotten about the momentary feeling I'd experience going down Stan's steps and praying I didn't fall in them. By the time I made it to the hostess stand, I was just glad I'd made it out alive to take on my next test: joining my friends at our table without alerting the hostess that they'd lied to her when they said their whole party was there.

I quickly scanned the room, looking for their spot. The key was to not make it look like I didn't know where I was going. If I was going to pull this off, it had to seem as if I'd simply stepped out for a second (to take a call, honest!) and was returning to my seat. Any inference that I was looking for the table would give me away in a heartbeat.

Thankfully, it took me less than a minute to find them, tucked off in the left corner of the lounge, all three of their heads tilted back in riotous laughter and their cocktails halfway drunk down. *So much for getting here before their drinks arrived.*

Using the phone as the prop for my ready-made excuse, I slipped past the hostess, who gave me a knowing look, and strutted up to the table. Magically, the waiter arrived at the same time with my two glasses of tequila and club soda and a separate plate of lime quarters.

I accepted this latest round of Stan's miracles, plopped down into the seat that they were saving for me and took a big swig of tequila before ever saying a word. Conspicuously, the laughter had all stopped as they watched me gather myself in their presence. When I was settled in, I finally broke the silence.

"Hi, ladies, sorry. I know."

"Six forty-five, *cher.*"

"Hey, you were supposed to be playing good cop. Was that only over text?" I asked Reagan.

She threw up her hands in mock protest. "No, no… I'm just noting the time."

"I know, and I apologize. It's just…been a day." I took another swig of the tequila. If I wasn't careful, I'd be done drinking it before I even added the soda and lime to it. "But I'm here now! Please don't be mad at me. Just love on me and tell me all that's been going on in your lives."

"We could never be mad at you," said Robin. "We love you—you know that. Now, those kids, though? That's something different."

"Touché."

"Before we fill you in, we ordered the usual—fried wings, catfish nuggets, mozzarella sticks and potato skins. Did you want anything else?" asked Reagan. "Like another drink, maybe?" She pointedly raised her eyebrow at my half-drunk glass of just the tequila.

"I told y'all. A day! But no, I've been daydreaming about their mambo sauce for several hours. So, I just hope it's a ton of wings."

"Of course. Have we met? Hi, I'm Robin, lover of flats and whole wings, not drums, and mambo sauce connoisseur." Robin put out her hand as if she was getting ready to shake mine on a first meet.

"Okay, okay. I get it. Now fill me in. It looked like y'all were rolling on the floor laughing when I walked in. What's going on?"

"Oh my God," Robin began. "Rae and I were talking about our two failed dates so far. And I was just telling them about the guy who took me to the African American history museum—"

"The Smithsonian National Museum of African American History and Culture, thank you very much," Reagan interjected.

"Right. All those words," Robin said, jokingly rolling her eyes. "Anyway, so the date's going well, right? We started in the cafeteria and ate some of that amazing soul food they have there, me and dude are talking, getting to know each other. I'm laughing. His teeth are sparkling. The whole nine. So, then we get up and I'm thinking we're going to go down to the basement to start the Founding of America exhibit, right? Tell me why this fool goes, 'Yeah, I was thinking we could stick with the Baldwin exhibit or maybe even the sports jont.'" Robin normally wove through her stories like she could have been a teacher, and tonight was no different. She even made sure to give the unnamed guy his own deep-toned voice and DC-laced vernacular, where "jont" meant "one."

"Now, I'm all for both of those exhibits, but something feels off, so I say, 'Sure, but what's up? You worried that the parts about slavery and Jim Crow are going to make you get too emotional in front of me? I'm a crier, so I don't judge.' You know, like, joking with him, right?"

"Right, right," Reagan and Rebecca egged her on, clearly already knowing the punch line but waiting for me to hear it.

"He says, 'Nah, that's not it. I just don't subscribe to all that mess they try to teach us about slavery.' Now, my ears are perked up, I'm standing up straight and I'm partially intrigued but also disgusted. There I am, standing in front of this amazingly bronzed, cocoa butter, dipped in the Sahara–type brother, and he's telling me he doesn't believe the transatlantic slave trade happened? Couldn't be! But I was. He really didn't believe it and was convinced it was the just the man's way of trying to keep us down by teaching us that we were slaves and not kings."

"Wait, what?!" I was floored and almost reached for my tequila glass again but caught Reagan's raised eye. I switched course, poured my club soda in finally, squeezed a lime, swirled the glass around and then took a sip.

"That was the exact reaction we had," said Reagan, giving me a wink. "Wild, right? Because also, who brings someone to *that* museum, in particular, when you don't think Black people were enslaved in America?"

"Yeah, no clue. But now we know to ask this on first dates, Rae. Like, sorry, before we proceed further, you believe slavery happened, right?"

"Well, now you have me wondering if I need to ask Nick!"

"No, don't do that to our Nick. You would know if he was foolish like that after three years. Trust me."

"I hope so!"

"What about Oliver? He believes slavery happened, right?" Robin asked Rebecca.

"He better! But also, I feel like I might be out of my element a bit here," Rebecca answered, her face flushed with relief as the waiter came back to our table with our food. Normally, I would have joined her excitement, ready to inhale the wings immediately, but I wasn't letting her get away with that comment so easily.

"Wait, why's that?" I asked.

"I mean, because you know, I'm...white." Her last word came out like a whisper, as if she was getting ready to say a curse word to her friends in church and didn't want the pastor to hear.

"What?! Since when?" I grabbed my chest and clutched my nonexistent double strand of pearls for emphasis. "Reagan, how could you not tell us? All this time I thought she was just one of your Creole relatives!"

"Okay, okay. I'm not saying it's a secret that I'm white," Rebecca countered, clearly getting my dramatic sarcasm. Off to the side, I could see our waiter holding in his giggles and pretending not to eavesdrop on our exchange. "I just...am not trying to center my experience as the white person in our friendship. That's all."

"That's great, *cher.* But all we wanted to know is if Oliver was a white hotep or not. You're good. Breathe," Reagan laughed and passed her a plate with a catfish nugget on it.

"You're right. I'm sorry. I was totally overthinking. And God, I hope he isn't."

"Better not be," Robin blurted out right before she stuffed a potato skin in her mouth.

"Speaking of Olly," Rebecca started, once again visibly comfortable enough to join the conversation.

"All of these dating stories had me thinking about the first time he and I went to a sex club."

"Wait, how is that the same, Becs?" Reagan asked in between bites.

"Because! We've been together so long that I can't remember first dates anymore. But going to your first sex club is *like* going on a first date. You don't know what's going to happen. You hope it's fun. You're equally prepared to bail in twenty minutes and hoping it's worth getting dressed up and that you end up staying for at least a few hours."

"Okay, I'm actually following you now," said Robin. "Proceed."

"So, right…so, Olly and I hit up our first sex club about five years ago. We were both extremely nervous but trying not to let the other know. Poor Olly, though, at one point, I grabbed his hand, and it was so sweaty it felt like I'd submerged it in dishwater. Outside of that, he was doing a great job of remaining calm. That's until we get there, and each time someone comes up to us, he shouts out, 'This is my wife. I love her.' You should have seen their faces," she said, pausing to catch her breath from laughing hysterically at her own story. "Each time, the person would slowly turn back around then bolt away from us as fast as they possibly could. At a certain point, I had to just be like, 'Oliver, I love you, too. But maybe we're not ready yet. And that's okay.'"

"Wow, I bet he felt so reassured," replied Reagan.

"He really did. And then, the next time we went—"

"It was on and poppin'!" Robin interrupted.

"Yeah, something like that," Rebecca said, chuckling a little.

"I love that, though," said Reagan. "I always say what I love about y'all is that you figure out what works for you two and you do that. Everyone else be damned. That's what me and Rob are trying to find with this date pact, but whew, it's rough out here."

"What?! You were just in the dating game a few months ago, before you and Jake got back together. You haven't been out long enough to have forgotten that the pickings are slim," Robin said, laughing.

"Correction. I was in the friends-with-benefits game, occasionally dated a bamma or two here and there, and then got tricked by Luke. That is not the same."

"Ugh, Luke," we all said in unison.

"I know. I know," she said, rolling her eyes. "But the guy I went on the date with last night was not much better…"

Reagan began recounting her date and telling us how they'd gone to get ice cream, but it turned out that's where he brought all his first dates. A fact that she realized when the staff started giggling how he was back with "another one." But as she continued talking, I could suddenly feel tears starting to well up in my eyes, slowly, and then all at once, like a trash-can fire that couldn't be contained. Once again, I was sitting around my friends, listening to them tell all these fantastical stories, and what did I have to contribute? Some kid who threw paint at the walls today? Even if they had asked me what made me so late, which they didn't, how thrilling was that story going to be? It certainly didn't compare to the first time Becs went to a sex club with her husband or the Black guy who didn't believe that a large proportion of Black Americans had been enslaved.

I cleared my throat and reached for some food, hoping that the act of eating might distract me from the unhappy and invisible feelings creeping up my throat and desperately trying to claw their way out. It was like my body and brain were betraying me when I needed them the most. All I wanted to do was sit down and enjoy some good food and drinks and laugh with my friends, but *nooooo*. Instead, I was on the verge of ugly tears while they were all having the time of their lives. I laughed when they laughed to not draw attention, but I was no longer listening to what any of them said.

I was also equal parts thankful and frustrated that no questions had been directed my way in the past ten minutes, so no one even noticed how I was completely in another world from them. I vaguely heard one of them say something about how much they liked it when a guy grabs a butt cheek and kisses you passionately at the same time, and that was another reminder of the lackluster sex life I was also experiencing lately. Tears threatened to crash to the surface again, and I bit my tongue to hold them back.

How was it possible I could feel so alone among the people who most felt like home?

Five minutes later, my plate was empty again, Robin was telling a story about the prince and I was ready to get the check to leave. My eyes were burning from the tears I held back, and I thanked whoever was in charge of all these Stan's miracles for them not just flooding to the surface and ruining everyone's evening. I grabbed my phone out of my work bag as my next distraction attempt and instinctively clicked to Nick's name.

I miss us, I texted. I miss the romance and spontaneity in our relationship. I pressed Send before I could overthink it and psych myself out from this moment of honesty.

He responded in less than fifteen seconds.

Nick: What do you mean? We have both of those in droves.

Me: We used to. Not anymore.

Nick: I don't know what you're talking about, Jenny. I'm doing the best that I can.

Me: I know. That's what I'm worried about.

Nick: What does that mean?

Look, can we talk about this tomorrow when we see each other?

Feels like text isn't the right venue for this conversation.

Me: No, you're right. It's okay.

I was extremely conscious of the fact that I was once again reassuring him instead of advocating for what I wanted.

Me: I'm out with the girls anyway. It's fine.

Nick: Okay.

Are you okay?

Obviously not, I thought. *Or we wouldn't be having this discussion.* I didn't text that, however. I just said what I always say: Yeah, I'm fine.

Nick: Okay, love you. Text me when you're home.

Me: Love you, too.

It took everything in me not to jump out of my seat, slam my phone down on the table and go running to the bathroom to scream and cry. Instead, I put my phone back into my bag, calmly asked Reagan to order me another drink and then walked to the bathroom like a normal person who hadn't just had her boyfriend crush her heart in the span of fourteen texts between the two of us. I walked inside with just enough time to close a stall door and break down into a silent cry.

By 9:43 p.m., I was back in my seat and had pulled myself together enough to join in the conversation and laughter with my friends—for real this time.

At eleven, I decided that maybe Robin was right and a therapist was something I should consider. At the very least, it couldn't hurt.

The clock was striking midnight when we were walking out of Stan's, full and tipsy enough for me to ask Robin for her help.

"We really don't know what happy hour means," she was saying to no one and everyone as I approached her. "Good thing Oliver trusts you, right, Becs?"

"It definitely helps that we have an understanding!" She raised an invisible glass in the air to toast her marriage to her husband who wasn't with us. *Yep, we were all toasty.*

"Rob?" I said, quieter than I intended.

"Hmm?"

"You think you could give me some therapist suggestions sometime next week? After today, I don't know, I just feel like I need someone to talk to who's not the three of you or my mom. No shade."

"None taken. Truly," she said, tilting on her heels as she tried to cup my chin in her hand. "You got it, doll. I'll send you a name before the end of the weekend."

When Robin was reverting to calling people by pet names, I knew we were maybe even more than toasty. I was probably going to have to remind her, but at least I'd taken the first step.

"Thank you. Genuinely."

She leaned in and gave me a big, long hug, pressing her bosom against mine to try to give as tight a squeeze as she could.

"Thank you for trusting me with this ask. You think I didn't see you space out for a time tonight, but I did. I just didn't want to call you out. But I think this will be a good thing." She squeezed me tight again for emphasis, and it almost burst my tears out of my sockets again.

"I love you," I whispered back.

"I know. And the feeling is very mutual."

As we let go of our embrace, all our Ubers pulled up one after the other. Like we were almost programmed to do at this point, we each checked the license plate numbers and then climbed in, ready to be whisked off to our homes, where we'd inevitably peel off our clothes, curl up in bed and be asleep in less than fifteen minutes. Well, everyone but Rebecca. Who knew what Oliver had waiting for her when she got home? He was either going to be knocked out already or he'd do something like have a note with instructions for her to get undressed and slide handcuffs on herself. No in-between.

The last thing I heard before my car pulled off was Reagan screaming out of her back seat window.

"Don't forget to text when you're home safe!" she shouted to us and everyone else leaving Stan's that night.

I smiled at her consistency, sat back in my seat, closed my eyes and prepared to enjoy my seven-minute ride home. I'd been rushing or holding back feelings all day. This was going to be a time when I could finally sit back and relax...and just breathe.

Chapter Seven

Sitting in the therapist's waiting room five days later, I caught myself anxiously tapping my foot on the carpeted floor. My brown pointed-toe ModCloth flats with heart-shaped white polka dots were the perfect contrast to Diane's heather-gray shag rug, but I could feel my body looking for any reason to bolt out the door before she could come into the waiting room and introduce herself. The tapping was my clue that, even though I'd only checked in a minute ago, my feet needed to move soon—either out of the building or into her office, but somewhere and ASAP.

Diane Cooks was one of five names that Robin sent to me over the weekend, but she was the only one who had an opening after school the next week. It also helped that she seemed to be a Black woman in her early forties, so I figured she was young enough to understand what I was going through, but old enough to no longer be in the thick of it like I was. Her website noted that she was originally from Long Beach, California, went to Spelman College for undergrad and Tulane University for grad school, and then followed a path that led her to DC and George Washington University for her PhD. I could appreciate a Cali chick like myself who went to an HBCU, so I was hoping this would be a good sign for us.

Two minutes later, I saw this slender woman walking down the hallway toward me. Her hair was impeccably coifed in what looked to be shoulder-length, auburn faux locs, but they were done so immaculately I thought for a second that they were real. That was until I remembered the photo on her website, in which she was rocking the perfect silk press. A woman who liked changing up her appearance? I liked her already.

She said goodbye to her last client with a gentle touch on his shoulder and then turned her attention to me.

"Jennifer?"

"Yes," I said standing up and simultaneously holding my hand out to shake hers. "Diane, right?"

"Yes. It's so nice to meet you." We shook hands, and she motioned for me to join her back down the hallway. "My apologies for the delay. My last session ran over just a little, but I hope you had some water while you waited?"

I looked behind me, and only then did I notice the water and tea station with glasses, mugs, an expensive-looking machine that I assumed spouted out cold and hot water, various teas, lemons, sugar, and honey. I'd completely missed that as I waited, focusing my attention only on the carpet and the front door.

"I didn't, actually. But maybe next time."

"Ah, okay. Understood." She looked at me knowingly and gave me a kind smile. "Well, there's water in my office as well if you get thirsty."

When we reached her office, it was sort of everything I expected it to be, and yet slightly different. On the left side sat a sofa that took up most of the wall but was unexpectedly a burnt orange. Next to that was a simple circular side table that held a box of tissues, a water pitcher, two glasses and a succulent. The table was a dark mauve color, weirdly contrasting perfectly with the electric blue rug underneath. On the other side of the sofa was a simple gold bookshelf that featured James Baldwin and Toni Morrison books, an air purifier and essential oil diffuser, and more plants. And then her chair faced it all, positioned diagonally on the right.

"You were expecting muted colors, right?" she asked me, watching my eyes float over the various aspects of the room.

"Ha-ha, yeah, maybe so."

"I'm not really a muted-color kind of person." Diane shrugged and sat down in her chair, motioning for me to do the same on the sofa. "So, tell me, Jennifer, what brings you here today?"

"Honestly," I began with a sigh, "I'm normally the positive energy friend, right? But lately, I have been on the verge of tears or actually crying, like, all the time."

"Hmm. Can you tell me more about this?"

"I don't know. I just don't feel like myself. I mentioned to my closest friends that sometimes I feel like I'm being left behind. I see the amazing—or even just wacky—things going on in their lives, and I look at myself and feel like a side character in my own storyline. I've had the same job for years. And while I love my students, I feel like I could be doing so much more with my psychology/English double-major degrees than teaching third graders basic geography, you know? But I don't know what that looks like if I'm not in the classroom. My relationship suddenly has no spark in it, and I'm worried that it's either something I did or that Nick is just so comfortable now that he has no interest in doing the passionate things that I once thought made us 'us.' And if either of those are true, what does that say for us? Are we really as built to last as I have believed the past three years?

"On top of all that, one of my best friends died earlier this year, and I'm not sure that I fully grieved her. Sure, we cried at and after the funeral, and we've commemorated her as we've traveled together or just hung out at each other's apartments. But there are times when my whole body aches from how much I miss her. And then, the other day, I realized that since she passed, I'm the only non-*R* name left in our group! I mean, how much more on the nose can life be?"

I slumped my shoulders down, having released all my thoughts in rapid-fire succession. I half expected to look over and see Diane either in shock or furiously writing down how crazy I was in her notebook. She was doing neither. Instead, what I caught was a face filled with compassion and someone leaning closer to me in her seat.

"That seems like a lot of thoughts you've been holding in for quite some time."

"Yeah, I guess so."

"How does it feel to say those things to me?"

"It feels… Honestly? Like a big weight was lifted off my chest." I breathed in deeply for the first time in days and sat back into the sofa.

"That makes sense. Sometimes we just need to say how we're feeling, with no judgment or attempt at understanding. Just release everything that's haunting us. Is this the first time you have verbally articulated these feelings?"

"All of them at one time?" I asked with a nervous chuckle. "Yeah, definitely."

"Well, what do you think has stopped you before?"

"I guess a lot of it feels so immature and selfish. Like, great, I'm the person staring down thirty and feeling as if I haven't done enough with my life. Welcome to the basic club, Jenn." I rolled my eyes and instinctively lifted my right hand to my head to massage my temple.

"You think it's basic to miss your friend who died?"

"Well, no, not that part. But everything else? Maybe?"

"Hmm. So, I am of the belief that all our feelings are valid," Diane said as she finally sat back in her chair. "Not just the ones that society says are okay, like grief. But also, feelings of loneliness, comparison, shame, disappointment... Do any of those resonate with you when I say them out loud?"

My eyes welled up, a familiar sensation for the past several months. This time, however, I didn't have the strength to hold them in. The tears came pouring down my face before I could even reach for the tissue box that sat near the sofa in arm's reach.

"All of them," I said quietly.

"Then, they are all valid and worthy of exploring, Jenn...are you okay with me calling you Jenn? I noticed you called yourself that when talking."

"Yes, please, do." I cleared my throat, unsure if she could hear any words coming out of my mouth, because I was so awestruck from finally being seen by someone who just wanted me to be okay.

"Okay, good. So, then, Jenn, let's start with you saying that you don't feel like yourself and you feel like you're being left behind. How long have you felt like this?"

"Wow, I don't know, honestly. For a while now. The easy answer probably has something to do with me turning thirty at the end of the year, but it didn't start just this year. It feels heavier now, though."

"Explain heavy to me."

"It just feels… I don't know, like I'm constantly walking around with my chest tight, my body tense and on the verge of tears at all times. I'll be out with my friends, drinking and laughing, and stopping myself from crying at the same time. The other day I was lying in bed with my boyfriend, and tears started rolling down my face."

"Well, I think it's clear that you have a lot of sadness that needs to be resolved. And maybe the heaviness you feel is because you keep holding back your tears. Have you ever just given in and allowed yourself to cry?"

"Sometimes? I mean, I went into a public bathroom the other day and broke down. Does that count?"

"Maybe." She shrugged her shoulders sort of casually. "Did you feel any sort of release after that?"

"Not really. Mostly just embarrassment and fear that something was seriously wrong with me. It's what prompted me to make an appointment with you."

"Okay, well, I'm glad you made the appointment. But I'm sorry to hear that you had such a hard experience." Diane looked at me with the compassion of an older sister or a cool aunt. Somehow, she still wasn't taking any notes, just listening to me. I guess I had the idea of a therapist completely wrong in my head; all this time I'd pictured someone meticulously taking notes and looking at you over the rim of their glasses as you spewed your heart out. "Let's go back to you saying that it feels heavier this year. Why this year?"

"I think I've always felt a little left behind. My closest friends have these really high-powered jobs, my boyfriend is making big moves as an accountant at his firm and I'm a teacher—a really important job, of course, but I've been wanting to do something more than that for a few years now. And this year, it's like everything piled on top of those feelings. Christine died. Nick started working more, and so our relationship has kind of suffered because of it. And I just looked up and all of a sudden didn't really know where I fit in anymore."

"Let me ask you something. Are you unhappy with your job because of the job or because you don't think it lives up to what your friends are doing?"

"Both, I guess." I squirmed around on the sofa a bit, suddenly uncomfortable with the thought that I was letting my friends' lives dictate my happiness. "I mean, I don't feel like I'm doing all that I can be doing. But I'd be lying if I didn't also think that my life in comparison with my friends was hashtag boring."

"Okay, that's fair. There's no judgment here. I just wanted to start understanding where your unhappiness stems from."

At the word *unhappiness*, my eyes started burning again with tears that wanted to fall. I reached for another tissue to blot my face and maybe even hide my shame a bit.

"Tell me what's happening right now," Diane asked, leaning in closer to me again. I had a feeling that if she wasn't my therapist, she would have come over and given me a hug. Not sure why I felt that, but it gave me some comfort. "What are you thinking about that prompted these tears?"

"I guess just hearing you say I'm unhappy. That someone would see me like that and not judge me. It just... I *am* so unhappy these days..."

"I want you to know that I'm never here to judge you. I may challenge on you some of your thinking, but if you ever feel like I'm judging you, I want you to feel empowered to tell me that. Deal?"

"Deal."

"Okay, now, how do you feel about us continuing to explore these feelings in future sessions? Is that something you'd want to do?"

"Definitely." I wasn't quite sure how long I'd been talking, but I was amazed at how this woman had gotten me to open up so quickly. Something inside me knew I wanted—no, needed—to see her some more.

"Great. I'm glad to hear this. Because we have a

lot to touch on. What kind of schedule do you think you can commit to going forward?"

"Maybe once every two weeks for now? I know I probably need more than that, but—"

"Jenn," Diane interrupted me. "What I hope you learn pretty quickly by working with me is that I'm not at all interested in what we or 'people' think we should be doing. I'm interested in working with you to feel like you are at your best, to be comfortable expressing your feelings to your friends and loved ones, and to being honest and gracious with yourself about what you need. And that includes things like how often you see me. Does that sound good?"

"That sounds great."

"Okay, so I have some thoughts about what I want you to do before we see each other again in two weeks. Now, if you don't finish all of these, that's okay. It's not a test. But I think it might help our next conversation progress further. You down?"

"Let's do it," I said, eager to hear what she had to say. I sat up fully on the sofa and brought my calves underneath me into a cross-legged position.

"Great. So, there were a few things I noticed when you were talking. The first is that it seems that you compare yourself to your friends a lot. I think you know this, and that's okay—it's something that we all do. But when we only compare ourselves to what we see as good in their lives, it can be a setup for beating ourselves up for not living up to the fairy tale we've imagined their life to be, and then deep disappointment. I would like you to lean into what you love about your friends so that instead of comparing yourself to them, you can draw inspiration from them. This can look however you want it to."

"Okay, that sounds good." Sensing more directions were coming, I leaned over to pull my phone out of my work bag and began quickly typing into my notes app.

"I also want you to take some time and take an honest look at your life to determine what, if any, changes will make you happier. Maybe this can be journaling on some ideas? You mentioned that you were a teacher and an English/psych major, so it could also look like writing a creative story about Jenn being happy and noticing what elements come up when you develop this vision. You don't need to do this before we meet again, but it's something to start considering."

I typed furiously into my phone, only looking up quickly to nod and acknowledge I was agreeing to the second item.

"And the last thing is, have you talked to Nick about your concerns?"

"Well, what do you mean by talk?" I asked, finally putting my phone down to sheepishly look back at Diane.

"I mean, have you had a verbal conversation with him about the doubts you are having and your need for passion in your relationship?"

"Hmm, not really, I guess. I sent him a text last

week when I was out with my friends telling him that I missed us. But I think he just thought I was drunk texting him."

"Why do you think he thought that?"

"Because I told him that when I saw him the next day?" I put my head down in shame. "I know that wasn't the best thing to do… I just— He's such a good guy, Diane. I never want him to think I'm saying otherwise."

"That's okay. He can be a good guy, Jenn, and still not be giving you what you need to feel secure and validated in your relationship. But also, if you're not opening up to him, you're not giving him a chance to fix it. That's not fair to you or him." She looked me in my eyes, I guessed to make sure I was listening closely to that part. I was, but I also knew this might be the harder of the exercises she was asking me to do.

"So, I want you to talk to Nick about your feelings. It doesn't have to be some long, drawn-out, life-changing conversation. But he should at least know what you're dealing with. Okay?"

"Okay."

"Now, I'm looking at your face as we're talking, and I'm seeing some elements of fear popping up. Maybe we can take the last ten to fifteen minutes to discuss what has you nervous about working on these tasks until we see each other again."

Thirteen minutes later, I was walking out of the building, my phone in hand, and feeling slightly more like myself than I'd felt since probably the moment I heard that Christine had died. I breathed in the fresh September evening air and texted Robin.

Me: Hey. Loved the therapist. Thanks again <3

You free for a shopping lunch on Saturday?

Robin: Yes! I'm so glad you liked her.

And of course! Just tell me when and where.

Me: Let's do Georgetown. 2p?

Robin: You got it. I'll be there.

Part 2

"When I'm feeling a little low, I put on my favorite high heels to stand a little taller."

—Dolly Parton

Chapter Eight

One of the things I always admired about Robin was her sense of fashion. If she couldn't do anything else, the woman could style and dress her butt off. Not that I didn't have my own set of classic staples in my closet—I *was* rocking a cute pair of white Tory Burch flats, ripped jeans and a one-shoulder white tank top that tied at my waist to meet her to go shopping—but Robin was the ultimate chic expert. She always found ways to accentuate her long, thick thighs and her blond bob that bounced right on the edges of her shoulders. Since everything in my wardrobe felt like I'd seen it eighty million times, I knew shopping with her had to be my first stop on the "lean into your friends' strengths" tour.

Robin was also my best friend. In friend groups, that can be hard to single out sometimes, but with ours, it was pretty obvious. Reagan and Christine had come to college together, having known each other since high school, so there were times when it almost felt like they spoke a different language with each other. They'd start reminiscing about gumbo, po' boys and high school classmates, and that left Robin and me time and space to become just as close. Over time, we'd become the yin to each other's yang. She was the sarcastic, dry wit, but secretly a sweetheart girl from the Midwest, while I was the compassionate foil to her snark—the Sacramento girl who wore her emotions on her sleeve. With her, I felt comfortable letting my no-nonsense side out occasionally, and I helped her sometimes connect with what it meant for her to be vulnerable.

But Robin was also never on time unless it was for work. This was such a pattern of hers that we'd deemed her perpetual lateness RBJ time, short for Robin Bridget Johnson time. She was always one to five minutes late, not enough time to be super annoying, but just enough so that she could make her entrance into whatever building or venue she was meeting you at. It was the exact opposite of my incessant need to get to places at least five minutes early unless I was running late from work, which seemed to be my new normal lately.

Just like clockwork, Robin showed up, walking through the doors of Intermix at 2:03 p.m. wearing floral pants, a hot pink–crop top and flat nude mules on her feet. I already had in my hands a pair of coffee-brown pleather pants, some acid-washed jeans and a patterned gray skirt with a high slit on the right thigh.

"Hey, Jenny," she said, strutting up to me. "Sorry I'm late. Traffic was a nightmare."

Robin casually glanced around the store to determine what clothes Intermix had in stock, and I could see her eyes quickly scanning and assessing whether they were going to impress or disappoint her with their selection of clothing. Then she homed her attention in on me.

"Ooh, what do you have in these hands of yours?" she asked, already peeling them from my grasp. "This…" She held up the coffee-brown pants so that the indoor lighting sort of flickered off them. "This is the one. Don't you have a white button-down boyfriend shirt that you could tie at your waist and wear with these?"

"Yeah, I do," I responded, in awe of her fashion memory.

"Perfect. I feel like there's probably at least two or three other shirts I can think of offhand that you can pair with these, so you absolutely have to get them." She looked over the other options I'd previously had in my arms, and her face scrunched up disapprovingly.

"These, I'm not so sure of," she said politely, referring to the acid-washed jeans. "Do you love them?"

"I mean, I don't know. I'd just started browsing around while I waited, that's all."

"Okay, so that's a no."

She started walking to where I'd pulled the jeans from earlier in the store to put them back.

"The easiest way to get into a closet rut is to buy clothes or accessories that you don't love or that you can only wear with one other item. So, we're not doing that today." She winked at me to try to couch any inkling of coming off as bossy. It worked, of course.

"That makes complete sense," I responded, following her as she wandered to the back of the store to pick up a jumpsuit she'd spotted when she walked in.

"What about this?" She turned toward me and put the navy blue jumpsuit up against my body to make an assessment. "Do you like?"

"Yeah, I think it's cute."

"But do you love it?"

She waited for my answer, and I suddenly felt like I was being given a pop quiz in class.

"Mmm, I'm not sure I love it—"

Robin was already swinging around to put it back on the rack before I could finish my sentence.

"But I haven't even tried it on yet. I could love it once I put it on, right?"

"Maybe." She shrugged. "But it won't be on you when it's hanging in your closet, either. So why start with something that needs convincing?"

I nodded in agreement and wondered just how

many items I owned that had indeed started out that way. Probably far too many to admit.

Robin fingered her way through more clothing racks, intermittently stopping to assess items for us both and slowly but surely building two small piles in her arms.

"Okay, tell me more about the therapy session. I know you loved it, but like, what was it that you enjoyed?"

"I wouldn't say I enjoyed it, actually. I cried a lot."

She swung back around to me with sad eyes. "Oh, no—"

"No, but that was a good thing. I needed to cry."

"Oh, okay, phew! You had me worried there for a second."

"I know, but it's fine. But to answer your question, I think it just felt good to talk to someone. I know I have you guys, but this was different. It was like I didn't need to hide anything from her for fear that it might hurt her feelings or that I might feel embarrassed after saying it."

"I get that, for real. Obviously, we want to be able to think we can tell each other everything, but the reality is that sometimes you need a person not in the thick of your life to talk to."

"Exactly." I hesitated before saying more, but since Robin was my best friend and the person who recommended Diane to me, I decided to give a few more details. "We talked about Christine a little."

"Oh, yeah?" Robin asked, and I could see her

body tighten up just slightly. "I can't imagine that was easy."

"Not so much, no. But since she didn't lose her, too, I didn't have to spend the bulk of my time also comforting her, you know? I could just focus on how much I miss my friend."

"I hear you. My therapist and I talk about her a lot, too. And just how it always seemed like, despite all the times she had to be hospitalized, you still thought she was this miracle person who would pull through. Almost like we got used to assuming she'd make it every time…until she didn't."

"Yeah. I think also we saw Reagan go through this whole transformation of taking more risks and not focusing on perfection to be happy when Christine died, and I…went to London and Paris, came back, and was still just a teacher."

"Okay, but let's be real. Rae had already started that risk list before Chrissy died, and she's still a work in progress now—we all are. But this break with her and Jake is proof if you ever needed it that she didn't magically transform into a different person because her best friend died."

"That's true. I guess that would be kind of odd anyway," I said while picking up a green velvet button-down shirt and asking myself the "do I love it" question before ultimately putting it back. The pause in my focus gave me enough time to think about something else Robin had just said, too. "But wait, if you think it's just a break for her and Jake, why are you two doing the date pact?" I asked.

"Oh, that's easy! Because I support my friends, even when I think they're being ridiculous. And because I needed something fun to do after my breakup."

"That's fair. It's not like you loved Eric, but still, ending things with a prince can't be easy."

"Honestly, that part was really easy. Don't get me wrong, I had a blast when it was just the two of us, but I hated everything else about dating someone connected to the royal family. What was hardest was just that sinking feeling I had that I wouldn't find anyone else, and that I'm running out of time to do so. I needed to do something to erase those thoughts. So, voilà, let's go on beaucoup dates!"

Robin punctuated her voilà with a very theatrical twirl in the middle of the store, grabbing up a red ruffled skirt as she did so. This was everything I loved about my friend: drama, a touch of sarcasm, a pinch of vulnerability and somehow she still managed not to lose sight of the goal—shopping—while talking about herself.

"Oh, speaking of the pact, I have to tell you about the date I went on last night," she said, turning to me for a split second.

"Ooh, was it that good?"

"Absolutely not," she responded, laughing. "But at least it's a good story."

"Dang. Okay, tell me."

"So, we decided to meet at Barrel in Eastern Market, right? I get there, and he's seated at the bar waiting for me, dimples peeking out of his smooth, dark brown skin. I'm like, *yesss, he looks just like his pictures...this is great.*"

She paused for dramatic effect.

"Until I looked down and noticed his feet swinging from the bar stool." Her eyes bugged out, imitating how she looked when she saw the guy last night. "Now, it's not like I'm a heightist, but I'm five-nine—I'd at least like you to be eye level. This dude might have been five-five with lifts on. What am I supposed to do with that, Jenn?"

I laughed at the thought of Robin towering over her date and patting him on the head as if he was her little brother.

"So, what did you do? Don't tell me you walked right out."

"Of course not," she said, lifting a long-stranded gold necklace to my chest, silently asking me if it was a go or not. "I watched him hop off that damn stool and walk toward me looking like Kevin Hart's cousin, and I swallowed my pride as the host brought us to our table. After all that, this guy had the nerve to sit down and say, 'I guess you weren't lying when you told me you were five-nine.' Jennifer. Now that's when I almost got up and walked out. I mean, what woman lies about her height? Why would I do that?"

I chuckled at her story and nodded my approval of the necklace so that Robin could add it to my pile.

Once she was satisfied with my response, we continued walking.

"Anyway, that's how the night went. For the next two hours, he tried to make jokes about our height differences, and I just kept drinking to get through the cringe. Needless to say, I won't be seeing him again."

"Uh, yeah, I'm guessing not. Are you at least having fun with this pact, though?"

"You know what? I actually am. I know the stories sound ridiculous sometimes, but it's been a fun way to get back out there again. And at least I'm not at home wallowing over the prince that wasn't meant to be, right?"

"Ha. Very true."

"What about you? Are things any better with Nick yet?"

"Not yet, but Diane gave me some really good advice about us, so I'm hoping that will help. I may have some small jealous pangs when I hear your dating stories, but honestly, I have no desire to be back out there trying to meet someone new again. Plus, I love him. Something's just missing, and I'm hoping we can fix it together."

"Well, good. Because, let me tell you, dating is nothing to be jealous of." Robin looked down at our piles again and made an a-okay sign with her hands, signaling she felt like we had a good crop of items to pull from. "You ready to go try all these bad boys on so that we can see how much money we're spending before we eat?"

"Ha-ha. Sounds like a plan," I said, suddenly looking down at my pile of clothes and accessories and wondering what my damage would be. I had fewer items than I might have pulled because of Robin's system, but they somehow kept being the more expensive ones.

"Great! Oh, and I think Rae is going to join us for lunch, too. We didn't get a chance to connect after her last date, and I need the details."

"Perfect."

I followed Robin toward the dressing rooms, only slightly frustrated with the idea that my lunch plans might be taken over by stories from their most recent dates instead of being my friends' strengths tour. Still, slightly was progress, and I'd take it after only one therapy session.

"So, what's going on with your job? Why do you feel so bleh about it?" Reagan asked as we dug into our oysters, salads, crab cake sandwiches and cocktails at Sequoia—one of the restaurants seated right on the banks of the Potomac River along Georgetown's beautiful waterfront. The weather was nice enough for us to sit outside on the terrace, so we had unobstructed views of everything from kayakers and paddlers rounding the Key Bridge to the litany of mini-yacht-like boats docked in the river with the Kennedy Center in the background.

I slurped down an oyster before responding.

"Honestly, it's just—" I took a pause and sighed. "The more I do it, the more I know that I don't want to be in the classroom any longer. Don't get me wrong—I love the kids. But being a third-grade teacher is increasingly sucking the life out of me."

"Well, that's a vivid way of saying, 'I hate my job,'" Robin chimed in as she forked her burrata–heirloom tomato salad.

"Ha. And I guess that's a more succinct way of saying it. The problem is that I know what I don't want anymore, but I'm not sure that I know what I do want. Or if the kind of stuff I've been thinking about even comes with a job title that's an option at my school."

"There's always the option of convincing them to create a job for you," said Robin in between chews.

"You think that's possible?"

"Everything is possible."

Such a classic Robin answer. She'd been making her way through the finance industry, charting her own path for years. But education felt more traditional to me for some reason. I turned to Reagan to get a second opinion.

"Rae, what about you? How did you know it really was time to quit your last job, and then what helped you find the one you have now that makes you so happy?"

"To be honest? A lot of trial and error…luck… prayers. It wasn't one thing, but I knew I was so unhappy with what Peter was offering me that I just couldn't keep going at that job. It would have broken me. That didn't make it any less scary of a thing to do, though. That kind of leap always is."

"Mmm-hmm," Robin chimed in.

"Christine reminded me of that when I was complaining to her about how long it was taking for me to find something after I took my unorthodox leap. I can remember it like it was yesterday. She said, 'Leaping just means you have a greater chance for falling, but if you never step out of your comfort zone, you don't get the greater chance for soaring, either.'"

"Man, I miss her," Robin said, her eyes giving way to the sadness behind them.

"Me, too," I added.

"Yeah, it's really hard sometimes," Reagan said and then swallowed her bad feelings down with the food she stuffed into her mouth. She continued, "But y'all saw it, too. If it wasn't for the four of you showing up at my door the day that I quit to remind me that I'd done the right thing, I might have called Peter and begged him to give me my job back. And I would have been miserable today if I had done that."

"Yeah," I said, scooping up another oyster. I heard what they were both saying and agreed, but it still didn't make it any easier to figure out what I wanted to do.

"You know what also helped me?" Reagan asked

rhetorically. "I journaled my way through it. I sat down and wrote out everything I wanted in my next role, without worrying about what the title would be, and then made a commitment to myself to find that job and not settle for anything less. It was one of the most empowering things that I did at that time, and I really believe it led me to *SELENE*. Now I'm able to tell the stories I want to tell and shape the direction of the content in the magazine and the website. Do you know at least a few things that you'd want to do if money were not a concern?"

"That's a great idea. My therapist mentioned journaling, too, but I've mostly been focused on what I don't want."

"And that's good to know. But I think it's time to flip your perspective some. There's got to be at least two or three things you know you'd love to try."

"Hmm. That's true. Well, I know that I want to use my psychology degree more, and I'd love to be able to help with some of the behavioral problems we see with kids at the school who simply don't know how to express their feelings and so they act out."

"That's a great start," said Reagan.

"But… I know that I absolutely don't want to be a school counselor."

"Okay, okay. Also, good to know," she said, chuckling.

"You know what? As I'm thinking about this, I may start by making a list of the things I do as the third grade–level chair that I enjoy and see what it would look like to turn that into my actual job description. I know that I have a lot of creative curriculum ideas, but I'm just exhausted from trying to execute them on my own. And a lot of what I've started to do recently involves observing teachers and offering feedback, specifically on their behavioral health strategies with the students."

"Yes! Okay, now we're getting somewhere. All you have to do is keep writing out this list, and it will all start to come together, I promise. You'll be able to look at the descriptions and see if those match other education positions at your school—"

"Or other schools that you can use as leverage for Kendall," Robin interrupted. "Because, remember, you can always make the case that such and such school has this position, they need it, too, and you're the best person for it."

"So, so true." I sat back in my seat and took in the positivity I was feeling. "Wow, this is the first time I've been hopeful about my career in I can't even remember when."

"Ayee, that's what I'm talking about!" Reagan raised her glass high in the air, signaling for us to join her. "To bomb-ass, scary-ass, but totally worth it career decisions."

"And no friends left behind," Robin joined in, giving me her patented wink again.

"No friends left behind," I responded and then

took a huge gulp of my drink. "Now, Reagan, tell us about this week's date."

On my way home in my Lyft, I pulled out my phone and began jotting down more ideas in my notes app as we made our way from Georgetown to Bloomingdale.

Would love to:
- Inform curriculum that centers students and their emotional needs
- Work on behavioral management techniques with students
- Implement workshops, trainings and events to enhance school culture
- Give teachers practical classroom strategies to encourage positive behavior management

That seemed like a solid starting list. Only thing left was to begin researching what education jobs included those kinds of opportunities. I had no other real plans over the weekend, so I decided then that I'd take advantage of the lull in my event schedule and do some research. I was determined to see Reagan's and Robin's advice through to some sort of conclusion that made me happy.

As we rounded our way along Rhode Island Avenue and turned onto Florida Avenue, it dawned on me that there was one other thing I wanted to do this weekend—plan a romantic dinner for me and Nick tomorrow night where I'd finally spill the beans on how I'd been feeling about us lately.

Chapter Nine

The next day, I spent the bulk of my afternoon setting up my apartment to be a romantic oasis. Using string lights, fake eucalyptus vines, and tea lights left over from a party I'd thrown a couple years before, I decorated the entire apartment so that it almost resembled an Italian or Parisian café. I set up the dining table for dinner for two and cooked a white sauce seafood lasagna I learned from Reagan, as well as a tomato, cucumber, olive and feta salad, and popped open a bottle of prosecco for the night.

A few minutes before Nick was set to come through my door, I lit each of the candles and told Alexa to begin playing my Mellow Moods playlist, did a final check of my outfit, and was standing just off to the side when I heard him using his keys to walk in at 8:07 p.m. As he entered, Jill Scott's "The Way" coaxed him into the little escape I'd set up for us, and the smells of the food plus the candles hit him in all the best ways.

"Wow, babe. It smells and looks amazing in here."

He walked in a little farther, slid off his shoes and had just laid his eyes on me as Jill began crooning about the way her man loved her.

"Damn, Jenn."

Nick looked me up and down, pausing to take in my outfit—a pale pink spaghetti-strapped body-con minidress paired with my nude-and-gold linen Manolo Blahnik pumps—before proceeding farther. The outfit perfectly complemented my brown skin and slender curves, and I knew it.

"Hey, handsome," I said, finally walking toward him. "You like?"

"Uh, I don't think *like* is the right word."

I watched him as he tried to adjust himself without drawing too much attention to the fact that he was hot and bothered within just two minutes of walking into my place. It was the exact reaction I was hoping for, so there was no way I was letting up. Not after my last attempt went awry—though this time, despite what it looked like, I wanted us to talk before I fully seduced him. I slid my body right up to his and pulled him into a long, passionate kiss that started off slow but grew more and more intense as it went on. When I finally let him go, Nick looked like a kid who had just eaten too much cake but still wanted more.

"Are you hungry?" I asked.

"For food?"

"Ha. Yes, for food."

"Um, yeah, I could…uh…eat. The food does smell really good."

I turned around and let him watch me walk slowly to the kitchen, my booty swaying with the beat of the song, and feeling his eyes on me the whole way.

"You should have a seat at the table," I called out once I reached my destination. "I'll be right out with the food."

By the time I walked into my dining room with the lasagna dish, Nick was seated and had poured both of us glasses of the prosecco. It even looked like he'd had a glass all on his own while he waited. He'd also started to scoop some of the salad onto our plates. I sat across from him and finally decided to scale back some of my seduction so that I could focus his attention on the conversation that I wanted to have first.

"So, I know it probably seems like I'm setting up sexy time here—and there is certainly time for that—but really, I was hoping we could have a nice romantic dinner and just talk through some stuff."

"Whew. You mean you want me to be functional and have a conversation right now?"

"Ha-ha. Yeah. At least a little bit."

"While you're wearing that?"

"Maybe this was a flaw in my plan."

"No, no. It's okay. Let me just, uh…get myself together." Nick took another swig from his glass, looked me in my eyes as if that was the only place that he could look and be okay, cleared his throat, and was finally ready. "Okay, I'm good. Let's talk."

"Well, how was your day?" I asked as I cut into my portion of lasagna.

"Man, for once it wasn't too hectic. I had a lil' break from work, so I just met up with some of the guys to play basketball. I finally had a chance to look into volunteering with Big Brother Big Sister, took a shower, and then came here. Nothing too heavy."

"Oh, yeah, you've been saying you wanted to become a Big Brother. What do you think now that you did some more research?"

"I'm still not sure, to be honest. You have to really be committed to something like that, and with work being so busy lately, I wouldn't want to be in a position where I'm letting a kid down. I mean, you know, sometimes I can barely stay up when we see each other during the week."

"Oh, yeah, I know."

Nick raised a quick eyebrow at my monotone agreement but kept going.

"So, I gotta think about it some more. See if it's something I can realistically do."

"That's fair. I just love that you're being so intentional about it, you know?"

"You gotta be, babe. Gotta be."

"Well, speaking of intentional…" *Here was my perfect segue.* Or at least I hoped it was. Nick was getting ready to take a huge bite of his lasagna, but I knew if I didn't say what I wanted to say to him now, I'd eventually lose the courage to. "Part of what I was hoping to talk to you about was us being more intentional in our relationship."

"Oh, yeah?" Nick had a mouthful of food, but it was clear that I'd gotten his attention.

"Yeah."

"Okay, tell me more." He put his fork down and trained his eyes on me.

"Well, you know I saw the therapist on Wednesday."

"Yeah, my bad. We've seen each other since then, and I didn't even get a rundown from you on how it went."

"I thought it was really eye-opening, actually. We talked about leaning into my friends' strengths instead of comparing myself to them in negative ways. And yesterday, Rae and Rob helped me start thinking about what kind of job I might want outside the classroom."

"That's great, babe. I'm really happy to hear it's had that kind of positive effect on you already."

"Me, too, actually. But the thing is, we also talked about you. Well, us."

"Oh? As in something that is wrong with us?"

"As in I've been feeling lately like we're in a bit of a rut. And I think I've tried to seduce us out of it instead of just being honest with you and saying that I need more."

In the background, Luke James's "I Want You" began playing, just in time to break up the silence between us.

"You said it yourself, right? You're so tired when we're together that you're asleep within two hours some days. I try to get you to talk about it, but you don't want to, not in any real sense. And then I'm so unhappy with where I am in life. I think it's just made for a really bad combination for us." I paused before continuing and watched his face turn from supportive boyfriend to a hurt little kid, but I had to say what was on my mind even if that didn't feel good for him. That was something Diane had reminded me. "You took me on a brewery tour, Nick."

"I—"

"I know. It was your way of trying something different, but that's how I know I'm not the only one who thinks we're in a rut. That was a bad idea, but at least it was an idea. Something other than us sitting on a couch in front of the TV, eating delivery food until you pass out four nights a week. That's not what I want for us."

Nick sat in silence. I could see on his face that he was processing everything I was saying, but I couldn't tell whether that was in a good or bad way. Diane had said to come clean with him, but truthfully, I was scared I'd just ruined everything between us. After all, sitting across the table from me was an amazing, sensitive man who I knew loved me with every fiber of his body. And I'd just spent the past couple minutes telling him, *I know your job is kicking your butt lately, but I need more from you*.

After about a minute, Nick finally spoke. Just as Luke James was getting into his zone and hitting the really high notes of the song.

"That's a lot to process, Jenny," he sighed. "But I am thankful that you were honest with me. Come here." He gestured me over to him to have a seat on his lap.

I got up hesitantly but walked over to him and sat where my butt was positioned on his right thigh and my legs dangled over his left. I wanted so desperately for us not to be in this space, but I was thankful that Nick somehow knew what to do to comfort me through what had to be a really excruciating discussion for him, too. He placed his hands on my thighs before speaking again.

"So, you need more."

"Yeah. I just need us to be more intentional in expressing our love for each other again. You know?"

I searched his face for understanding and found his compassionate eyes staring back at me. This was why I loved him.

"I hear you. I don't like that you needed to say it. But I hear you. Work has been…a lot lately. And to be honest, when I'm with you, you are my refuge away from all the BS. So, I don't usually want to contaminate our space with whatever frustrations

I'm having at work. But I'll do better, I promise. With speaking up more and with reminding you how much I love you."

"Thank you, babe," I said, cupping his chin with my right hand and placing a soft kiss on his lips. Then, I quickly sneaked in a bite of my food before sitting back on his lap and placing my head on his left shoulder.

"But…there are days when I just don't have the energy to go on adventures with you across the city. I get that that probably makes me pretty boring, but sometimes there's nothing more that I want than to just fall asleep in your arms."

"No, Nick, I love that we have that—honestly, I do. It's just that when it's every night, with no deviation, no plans for travel, no spontaneous moments where you just grab me up and toss me across the counter… It just makes me feel like we've lost our spark and as if you don't desire me in a basic, sexual way anymore."

"Ha. Trust me, babe. I desire you in all the basic, sexual ways."

Nick grabbed a butt cheek to emphasize his point, which elicited a giggle from me.

"I love you. You know that, right?"

"I love you, too."

"And I'm only saying this because I want us to last."

"I know. Me, too."

"I also don't want to eat any more food."

"Oh, you don't, huh?"

"No. You see, I have this handsome, understanding boyfriend under my legs right now. So, about the last thing I have in mind is more lasagna."

"Well, that's good, because you…in this dress… on top of me? It's got me thinking of all the basic, sexual things I want to do to you right now."

"Yeah?" I leaned my torso close to his and put my lips on his without kissing him. Staring into his eyes, I simply whispered, "Tell me more."

"How about I show you instead?"

And with that, Nick grabbed the back of my neck, leaned my head back and kissed me like he needed air and I was the only one who could give it to him. Our lips still intertwined, I repositioned myself so that I was now straddling him, each of my legs on the outside of his. My dress rose above my butt in just the right way, and Nick grabbed the material so that it rested on my waist, completely exposing the black lace thong I had on underneath.

In this spot, I could fully feel his huge bulge growing bigger and heavier within his pants, desperate to break out and plunge inside me. But I wanted to experience the lust between us as long as I could. I wrapped myself around his chest, pressing my body into his and dragging my hands along his sculpted back. With each breath we took as we kissed, I could feel his chest pulsing and the muscles in his back and the sides of his torso getting tighter and tighter.

"Jennifer," he breathed into my mouth.

"Yesss."

My response was a whisper, a question and an answer all in one. "Yesss, what would you like?" and "Yesss, you can have me however you want right now." Nick took my answer just like I meant him to, and he suddenly rose his body up, lifting me along with him so that he was standing and my legs were wrapped around his waist.

Without another word, he strode to my bedroom, never letting go of my butt cheeks. Once inside my room, he laid me on the bed and began to take his clothes off, starting by unbuckling his pants so that he could release his penis from the agony of that kind of constriction.

"I want you to keep your eyes open, okay?"

"Yesss," I replied again. Another whisper and answer in one.

With the go-ahead response from me, Nick slipped his pants down his legs and around his ankles, keeping an intense stare on me the whole time. Next, he lifted his shirt up and began pulling it over his body. It took everything in me not to help him, but implicit in his request that I keep my eyes open had also been the notion that I was going to lie on the bed and just watch him, not participate. At least not until he said so.

With only his boxer briefs left, I took in desperate breaths trying to keep my composure. I watched him as the ankh tattoo on his chest lifted and descended with his inhales and exhales. I followed his hands as they went to his waistline and began pulling down the gray boxer briefs that partially contained the bulging organ that had been trying to get out for the past half an hour. As his boxers fell down his legs, it began jumping with quick syncopations, ready to be put to good use.

Once again, Nick caught my eyes and smiled. He knew exactly what he was doing to me.

"Not yet, eager beaver. You didn't let me finish eating, so I need some of that first."

His eyes went straight to my thong-covered vagina, and I could feel my juices starting to leak out as his gaze turned to me in the same way I'd been watching him. With a sort of primal groan, he grabbed the thong at my hips and slid it off my legs, tossing it somewhere into the ether of my bedroom. His touch was soft at first, but then he dived his head right in, lapping up everything he'd just elicited from me. By the time he clenched his lips down onto my clit, I was already feeling the tingling start of an orgasm. It grew from my toes and went up my body until I could no longer hold it in, and I exploded into his mouth.

Nick looked up at me and smiled again, licking his lips slowly to show me that he enjoyed it as much as I did. He couldn't possibly have, however, since my thighs were still twitching when he leaned over, grabbed a condom from the drawer we kept them in and then slowly inched his way inside me. I reached out and held on to him as I felt him opening me up, and then his stroke begin to intensify.

Wave after wave hit my body as Nick jointly performed figure eights inside me and our tongues twisted around each other. It was all I could do to hold on to his shoulders so that I didn't lose myself too much in the ride. And just when I thought I couldn't possibly take any more, Nick flipped me over onto my knees, grabbed my dress from the waist and pulled it up over my shoulders and head to fully reveal my body to him. I arched my back and positioned my butt in the air, prompting Nick to lick and kiss his way down my spine as he plunged into me from behind.

"Count down from ten," he whispered into my ear.

"Ten, nine, eight…"

With each number I counted, he kept up his stroke, and my orgasm climbed deeper and deeper until I had to let it out at "two." At what would have been "one," Nick crashed into me and exploded into the condom, both of our bodies going limp and falling onto the bed.

"You think that's a good start for more?" he asked between heavy breaths.

I could barely speak—just nodded while curling my body under his.

Chapter Ten

"Well, that sounds pretty spicy to me already," Rebecca said after listening to me recount my and Nick's steamy lovemaking session from two days before.

It was Tuesday after work, and she'd joined me at the National Harbor for a massage appointment at the Gaylord National's Relâche Spa. The appointments were a much-needed reprieve from work for us both and a convenient way for me to pick her brain about my latest Nick dilemma as we waited in the women's lounge.

The truth was that Rebecca was like no other friend I'd ever had. She was equal parts wild and untamed, a boss-ass IT professional, and one of the most genuinely sweet people you could meet. And best of all, she was unashamed about talking all things sex-related. Maybe it was because she was about five years older than the rest of us, or because she was a white woman who had privileges to be all those things at once; I don't know. What I did know was that of all the women I knew, she was the one who wasn't going to judge me for any sexual questions I asked of her. And I had many in mind.

"I know. It was fantastic," I said dreamily. "But it was also two days ago, and nothing has happened since then. I guess I just want to make sure it wasn't a onetime thing or that it won't be another six months before he practically devours me like that again."

"Jenn, two days?! Give the man's penis a chance to breathe."

"Okay, I know it sounds like I'm being dramatic. But it's been so long before this, I don't want things to go back to our normal from before."

"Sooo, you decided to hit up your resident polyamorous friend to get her advice on how to keep up the fiery part of your relationship?"

"Something like that. I'm not trying to tokenize you, though. I just figured you and Oliver are the polar opposite of a couple that's in a rut, so you might have some ideas."

"I'm just teasing." Rebecca relaxed her body and laid her head back in her chair before continuing. It was a great reminder for me to do the same—sit back and relax even while we talked.

Along with us, there were three other women in the lounge. Two had on their headphones, and one seemed to be engulfed in the book she was reading, so I was kind of okay speaking freely in public. Still, it had me slightly on edge extolling all the details of my sex life—and sometimes lack thereof—within earshot of others. I took in a deep breath and followed Becs's lead, relaxing my shoulders, unclenching my jaw and resting my eyes while I waited for her to say more.

"What do you want to know, exactly? Tips on keeping the fire alive? Recommendations on new things you two can try? Directions to my favorite sex club?"

Rebecca chuckled and paused, awaiting my response. Her brief halt in talking prompted me to reopen my eyes just long enough to see her slightly raised brow questioning how far I wanted this spicy advice to go.

"Any and all of the above, to be honest." I was a desperate woman clinging on to hope that what I experienced on Sunday wasn't an anomaly or a momentary harking back to a past time in my relationship, when Nick and I oozed sex whenever we were in close proximity. "It's no secret that part of what has kept your ten-year marriage thriving, Becs, has been your and Oliver's determination to not let your union feel stale. I just want to make sure that Nick and I stick to what we committed to at dinner."

"Okay, okay, I got it. How about we start off simple and then see if you need to raise the stakes later?"

"I'm listening."

"So, one of the things I love doing with Olly is leaving sexy and affirming Post-it notes where I know he can find them. I'll text him sometimes, too, but a text can imply that I want a response, and I don't always want that. These are mostly intended to be FYIs. So, for example, the other day, he put his hand in his pants pocket on the way to work and found a note that said, 'I can't stop thinking about the way you fit perfectly inside me. It's like we were created as one mold.' Then, he opened his work bag later in the day and saw another note that said, 'I love you so much. You are the partner I prayed for as a young woman.' And then on his way home, I sent him a text that said, 'I need you to ravish me tonight—screw me like the world is ending and only our love can stop it from crumbling down.'

"By the time he got home, no amount of exhaustion from work was competing with the kind of groundwork I'd laid. He walked in, immediately bent me over the sofa and consumed me for hours. Then, when we were done, we ate dinner and talked about how our days had gone like any other couple."

"Wow, that's so hot. You do that daily?"

"No, no. But I try to at least a few times a month. I like to make it seem random, so that he's not expecting it, but often enough that it's not completely out of the ordinary. And really, that's the key—Olly devouring me, to use your word from earlier, is normal for us. It's ordinary in the best of ways."

"Man, that's exactly what I want."

"And you can have it. You guys just have to find the stuff that works for you. It might not be exactly what Olly and I do—"

"No, I know. But I can certainly use the inspiration."

"Well, in that case, after this appointment, you should come back to my house for a second. I have the perfect thing for you—my pink, plush handcuffs. Olly and I have been using metal and rope lately, so we won't miss them right now. But if you haven't tried anything like that before—"

"I definitely haven't."

"Great. Then it's the perfect baby step in that direction to see if you two like a little BDSM or not. They're not really handcuffs, per se, because there's no lock on them; but it's the best way I can describe them. Truthfully, you can just slide them on and off your wrists, but it gives you the notion of being cuffed without any of the pain. You might call them little fuzzy wrist restraints, and you can use them on him, he can use them on you…whatever your little grasshopper heart desires."

I was more than intrigued with both of these suggestions and was just starting to fantasize about how Nick would respond to them when our names were called. Just as well—I didn't want to be the woman lying down on the massage table soaking wet as my massage therapist worked out the knots in my hips.

"Okay, so you're coming home with me, right?"

Rebecca and I stepped out into the chilly early October evening air, fully relaxed from our massages and walking with extra bounces in our steps.

"Yeah, definitely. As long as Oliver won't mind the impromptu company."

"Nah, he'll be okay. Plus, when he hears why you're there, he'll probably want to become your super sex saiyan. So, really it's more of a cautionary tale to you not to let my husband talk your ear off."

"I'll just let him know that I have to get over to Nick's for some very important business, so any more advice will have to wait."

"I know that's right."

We high-fived each other and began walking to Rebecca's car, which was parked on a side street near the hotel.

"What are you thinking of doing tonight?"

"I'm not sure yet, but your advice about the sext messages is making me think I should start by sending Nick a text letting him know that I'm coming over with a surprise and for him to be ready."

"Oh, yes, I endorse this. We should craft it while we're headed to my place."

By the time we reached Rebecca's black BMW and both climbed in, I was beyond excited for the rest of the evening. Once seated in her car, I pulled out my phone and began typing what I might send to Nick. I read it aloud to get Rebecca's feedback before pressing send.

Babe. I'll be at your place in less than an hour with a surprise…for you and Black Onyx.

"Wait, I'm sorry, who is Black Onyx?" Rebecca asked, unable to hold in her laughter after I read my drafted text.

"You know, his penis," I answered, much shier than I expected.

"That's what he calls it?!"

"Well, not anymore, but it's what he told me he used to call it when he was younger. I thought it would be kind of cheeky to use that, no?"

"Okay, no. Definitely not. Let's try again."

"Grr. Okay, how about this?" I erased my initial message and typed in another one before reading it aloud to Rebecca again.

Nick. I'll be by with a special surprise in less than an hour. *eggplant emoji*

"Not that, either! He's going to think you're bringing another man home." Rebecca was masterfully driving and laughing at my pitiful attempts to sext my boyfriend at the same time. Meanwhile, I was starting to get frustrated at how bad I was at it.

"How about this instead?" she offered. "Nick. I

can't stop thinking about how hot Sunday night was. I'll be over soon with a little surprise. Smiley face."

"Ooh, that's perfect. Let me send that now." I quickly erased my words and replaced them with Rebecca's, pressing Send before I could talk myself out of it. Then I put the phone down, took a deep breath, closed my eyes and hoped I'd get a positive response from him.

Within two minutes, my phone dinged and sent panic signals down my spine. I knew it was going to be Nick, but I was too nervous to turn the phone back over and look.

Out of the corner of my eye, I saw Rebecca notice my hesitation, and I sheepishly relented, picking the phone back up and pressing the side button to see my screen.

There it was a notification from Nick. A text that read simply, I can't wait. See you soon *tongue emoji*

Forty-five minutes later, I was kicking off my blue, teal and orange Ankara African print LeyeLesi oxfords at Nick's front door, the plush handcuffs behind my back in case Nick was sitting on the couch when I walked in.

To my surprise, he wasn't. In fact, I didn't see him downstairs at all.

"Babe, you here?" I called out after walking into his apartment and only seeing his work bag by the door as evidence that he'd been home that evening.

"Yeah, I'm upstairs. You want to just come up?"

"Okay, yeah. I'll do that."

I made my way up the stairs to his bedroom loft with great anticipation. There I was getting ready to introduce something new for us, and I was just hoping that Nick would be as into the idea as I was. Right before I reached the top, I felt my phone vibrating and checked it. It was a text from Rebecca.

You got this, Jenn. You are a sex goddess.

Clearly, she was great at sending texts to everyone, not just her husband. It was the perfect extra boost I needed. I hearted her text in response and then slid my phone into my back pocket, climbed the last two steps and almost drowned in my own spit when I saw Nick had a surprise of his own waiting for me. There he stood, balls out, penis hard and every muscle of his body bulging out, ready for action.

"Oh my God," I managed to eke out of my watering mouth.

"I figured two could have a surprise, right?"

"Absolutely."

Without another word, I walked up to him, slowly slipped my tongue into his mouth and ran my right hand along his torso. With the fake handcuffs still behind me in my other hand, I slid down his body until my face was right at his crotch, opening my mouth to take him all in. Gently at first, but then adding suction and flicks of my tongue as I continued.

Nick could barely keep his legs straight, so I moved my hands to the backs of his thighs to help hold him up while I kept sucking, bringing him deeper and deeper down my throat with only the sounds of my gagging to be heard over his moans. It was only then that he noticed the fuzzy object in my hand as it pressed again his skin while I gripped his left leg.

"Mmm. Babe, what's that?"

I momentarily released him from my mouth to answer.

"My surprise."

"Let me see." As he pulled me up to a standing position, his penis plopped out of my mouth, and spit dribbled from his head. That just made me want to get back down there even more. Instead, I indulged his curiosity and opened my hands for him to see.

"Rebecca gave it to me. She said it might be a good starter for us to try a little BDSM."

I couldn't tell if Nick was thrilled or shocked. He mostly just stood there for an excruciating beat while I contemplated how I might have just messed everything completely up.

"You talked to Rebecca about us?" he asked, his face finally revealing a little embarrassment and maybe some hurt.

"I mean, not really…just that I was interested in trying some new things. That's all."

"And she recommended handcuffs?"

"As a starter."

"Ha. Of course, as a starter." He threw his head back, but I still couldn't tell if the laughter was good or bad. "And this is something *you* want to try or something *she* wants you to try?"

"It's something I want to try—"

"I don't know about this, Jenn."

I could see him waffling, but I really wanted us to at least give it a shot. Looking Nick in his eyes, I attempted to reassure him.

"I think it could be fun. But, of course, only if you want to," I said, using my right hand to cup his chin.

"Okay."

Nick still looked a little unsure, but he took the handcuffs out of my left hand and quickly slipped one around that wrist. Then he raised my arms above my head with one hand and slipped my right wrist inside. With me fully at his mercy, he unbuttoned my pants and slid them down my legs, all while placing small nibbles along my thighs. Once I stepped out of the pants, he threw me onto his bed, flicked my panties to the side and began teasing me by just momentarily sliding inside me and then pulling out over and over.

"You want me to go deeper, right?" he groaned into my ear.

"Y-yes. I do."

"Sorry for you that you can't push me in right now with these handcuffs on."

He was right. I hadn't considered this aspect of being bound up. The thrill of being subject to his will was at once superseded by the agonizing reality that he could do whatever he wanted with me—he could tease me as long as he wanted to. It was extremely sexy. But it was also driving me up the wall, because the only thing I really wanted right then and there was for him to plunge into me so I could ride the wave of the orgasm I felt building in my body.

"Nick, please!" I cried out.

"Say it again." He was so close to my vagina but no longer in it, and I could see that he was enjoying the power he had to tease me. It was similar to the times when I would position my lips right on top of his and wait until he could no longer resist me and had to engulf my lips in his. The problem this time was that I had no way of doing the same to him. All I could do was beg.

"Pleeease. I need you now."

And with that, he finally gave in to me, slowly sliding himself into me. As wet as I was, I could still feel every vein as he entered, meticulously taking his time until he was as far as he could go. With one final thrust, Nick began pumping with full force, sending orgasmic chills up and down my spine. Since I couldn't hold on to his shoulders, I wrapped my legs around his waist, pulling him closer and closer to me, our skin slapping into each other as he continued stroking every inch of my insides.

"I love you, Jennifer Pritchett," Nick screamed out with one final blast, and we both came with a rocket sensation flowing between us.

"I…love…you…too," I mouthed between heavy breaths as Nick collapsed on top of me.

"Maybe your surprise wasn't such a bad idea after all," he said, rolling me into his body so he could wrap his arms around me.

"Definitely not."

He couldn't see the Cheshire cat grin on my face as he pulled me into his chest. But I was about the happiest girl on Planet Earth in that moment. My man fully and completely desired me. Maybe things were on the up and up for us after all.

Chapter Eleven

Three days later, Robin and Reagan were splayed out in my living room for a special Friday version of our bimonthly Nacho Thursdays, going over plans for our joint thirtieth birthday party. While both their birthdays had passed already—April 16 and June 30, respectively—we'd decided to have the combined party at the end of October for two reasons. One: since my birthday was December 14, we were looking for a time that wasn't right around any of our birthdays to make sure it really felt like a party for the three of us. And two, maybe more importantly, Howard University's homecoming was set for the last week in October, and we figured it was the best way to make sure the most people could attend.

But because we were throwing our bash during Howard's homecoming, we knew that our party had to live up to the famed HBCU's reputation. Howard parties were often known for being endless, full of the top fashions and laced with the best music and drinks, but during homecoming they were also packed with a mix of celebrities, students and young professionals. Even the *New York Times* once chronicled its legendary status, calling Howard's homecoming "a celebration of Black culture, a music and arts festival, a history lesson, a community reunion," and so much more. So, we couldn't leave any stone unturned for this semiformal affair. That meant renting out a bomb venue in the U Street area, making sure that we could have po' boys on the menu to honor what would have been the only ask from Christine if she were still alive, and, of course, ensuring that the drinks would be flowing all night.

Robin, ever the expert marketer, who was also low-key an event planner, found us the perfect spot that fulfilled all those asks: Harlot DC on the corner of Eleventh and U had the decor we wanted, the food we wanted (shrimp po' boys, house-made dumplings, black bean fritter tacos, shrimp and grits—yes, yes, yes, and yes!), the drinks we wanted, and the history of being located on the site of the renowned Bohemian Caverns. Now closed, Bohemian had seen my girls and many others partying the night away while we were in college.

"I'm so excited about this," Robin said, picking

up a nacho covered in black beans, cheese and steak. "I don't say this lightly, but I feel like this party is going to be *epic*."

"I don't know that I need it to be epic," I noted, leaning my back into the comfiness of my sofa. "I just want it to be fun, and sexy, and memorable—"

"Sooo…epic?" she questioned, interrupting me before I could continue offering up a ton of words to essentially mean the one that she'd already said. Robin sat on my love seat, her legs crossed at the ankles, but she leaned in closer to the coffee table to grab another chip as part of her emphasis on the word *epic*.

"Ha-ha, okay, maybe that is the right word," I said, conceding and pretending to throw my hands up in surrender.

Following that, I poured myself a glass from the margarita pitcher, trying not to overthink the remaining logistics too much. From what I could tell, we'd mostly finalized everything except our outfits, but one can never know what will come up last-minute with big parties.

"We have about two hundred RSVPs, and the venue can hold up to two hundred and fifty people, so that gives us wiggle room if some folks just randomly show up, which you know is possible," Robin continued after chewing.

"I can see it now—the two hundred and fifty-first person being my soul mate and getting turned away at the door," Reagan chimed in from the floor.

She'd sat there to be closer to the table, the food and the margaritas.

"Please. Unless that's Jake, I don't think you have anything to worry about."

Reagan feigned insult and put her hand to her chest like someone who had been called out of their name.

"I don't know what you're talking about."

"Oh, you don't?" Robin asked, very clearly referring to something I hadn't been brought up to speed on yet.

"Wait, what's going on?" I asked. "Did something new happen with Jake?"

"Well…" Reagan took a big gulp of her margarita and then another before speaking. "I may have seen him this week while I was out on a date with one of the pact guys."

"Wait, what?!"

"Mmm-hmm," Robin mumbled under her breath.

"Okay, let me tell you how it went down." Reagan sat up straight and turned her body toward to me. "I'm at Lost Society, right? And I look up from laughing at something my date said, and who do I see but Jake staring at me from the rooftop portion of the bar into where we're sitting."

"Wait, what?!" Clearly, my response wasn't changing the more I heard this story.

"I know, I know. Of all the places for him to be. And he was on a date! Like, the audacity to be dating in my city. You don't even live here."

"Well, he is here quite frequently, since his job is based in DC," Robin reminded her matter-of-factly.

"Whatever. He shouldn't be dating here. Date in New York, where *you* live." Reagan took another gulp of her drink, seeming to need it to finish the story. She was obviously upset, but I was ready to hear what happened that led Robin to still be on Team Jake. Reagan finally continued. "Anyway, it was so wild, almost like something out of a movie. Once we locked eyes, that was it. We were staring at each other the rest of the night. I can't even tell you what else the other guy and I talked about, because all I saw was Jake…on a date…with someone who wasn't me."

"That's…wow. I'm not even sure I know what to say." I was flabbergasted but also keenly aware that once again my friend had managed to put herself into the scene of a romantic sitcom. It never failed. And despite anything I did, I wasn't sure I'd ever be able to compete with that. Maybe that was a good thing? I still wasn't sure, to be honest, but I knew it was probably going to make for a good upcoming therapy session.

"Tell her the best part," Robin chimed in, jolting me out of my thoughts.

"Ugh. So, the thing is, we never said a word to each other. And I haven't heard from him since. It was just like this mesmerizing scene and then…poof! Nothing." Reagan dropped her head dramatically, as if what she'd just admitted amounted to giving up the secret code to a treasure or something.

"Wait, what?!" I really needed to come up with something else to say, and fast. But what else could I offer? The story she was telling just kept getting more and more ridiculous. Thankfully, my outbursts of the exact same words were more than enough to keep Reagan going.

"Right. And now Rob thinks he's going to show up at the party."

"I *know* he's going to show up."

"Did he say something to you?" I asked Robin.

"No. But I know these two. We all do. Reagan has had her fun with me and the date pact, but there's no way Jake is going to sit around and not do anything to get her back after seeing her on a date, under the stars, at Lost Society. You know that lighting they have does wonders for brown skin. I'm sure she was all aglow and he was plotting to get that thang back."

"So busy plotting that he never spoke to me."

"What did you want him to do? Leave his date and walk up to you in the middle of *your* date, dragging you out of there like Tarzan, screaming out 'mine'?"

"Of course not," Reagan rolled her eyes and grabbed some more nachos. "But some sort of acknowledgment would have been okay."

"Chile. The man couldn't keep his eyes off you. That's the acknowledgment." Robin took a sip of her drink with a face that said, *Trust me, I know what I'm talking about.*

"Wow, okay. I feel like I missed so much, and it's only been a few days since we talked."

"Well…" Robin sipped from her drink again. "I have some news, too."

"Did you run into the prince while on a date?" I asked, at first laughing but then stopping quickly. With these girls, that wasn't that much of a stretch to believe.

"Ha. Not quite. But I am thinking about moving back to London permanently and campaigning for a promotion to do so." Robin practically spit out her words, like an auctioneer trying to get them out as fast she could.

"Wait, what?!" I practically jumped out of my position on the couch.

"Is that all you have to say today?" Reagan asked.

"Well, you both keep leaving me speechless, so that's all I have!"

"I know. It's a lot to take in, but I'm really excited about the prospect. I felt like I was able to shine there at a level that I'm just not able to in the States, so I'm dying to get back. I will admit the one thing I'm worried about is whether we'll all be able to remain close if I'm all the way across the Atlantic Ocean."

"Please. As I told you earlier this week, that's what Zoom and flights are for," Reagan said, now positioning herself so that her back was flat on the front bottom panel of my couch and she could see both me and Robin in her periphery.

"That's right… Wait, you guys talked about this

already?" I wanted to be happy for Robin. I *was* happy for Robin, and Reagan, in a way that I probably wouldn't have been able to be just a couple weeks before. But there never would have been a time before the date pact when I would have heard that Robin was thinking about moving to London after someone else. It left me feeling slightly jealous, but I tried to remember Diane's words and lean into my friends' strengths. I closed my eyes briefly and shook off my feelings. The truth was that I was thrilled for both of my friends, so I refocused my attention back on that.

"Oh. Yeah, I mean, just during one of our date pact catch-ups," Robin responded, maybe noticing some of my unease at finding out after Reagan. "It came up as I was lamenting about how the dating hasn't gone too well for me so far, but that I was wondering if London might be a better fit."

"Ohhh, okay," I said, trying to reassure her that I was fine again.

I caught Robin searching my face, trying to see if I was upset, but I was insistent in not showing her any further disappointment from me. Both women had stepped up for me in the past couple weeks, helping me to shop and figure out what I wanted to do in my career. So, I could…no, I was *going* to be only hysterically happy for them. I leaned over and picked up the margarita pitcher from my coffee table, poured some more into my glass and then without asking, topped off their glasses as well.

"Well," I said, raising mine high into the sky. "I, for one, am overjoyed for you, friend. If London is where you want to be, I'm glad you were able to figure that out and that you're in a position to do something about it. That's the epitome of badass."

"Aw, Jenny!" Robin leaped out of her seat and lunged on top of me for a hug, almost knocking my drink out of my hand.

"OMG! I'm trying to give a toast here," I mumbled from under her body, my right hand still high in the air with my drink in it.

"My bad. But that moment deserved a hug first. Sorry. I'll compose myself. I'm just thrilled that you're excited for me." She jumped off me, but not before smacking a kiss on my cheek, and then went back to her spot on the love seat.

"As I was saying," I said, clearing my throat and jokingly rolling my eyes. "I am over the moon and stars for you, Rob. And this just means I'm going to have so many frequent flyer miles. Delta better get ready!"

"Wait, does Delta even fly internationally?" asked Reagan.

"Okay, not now, Rae."

"My bad." She ate a nacho, trying to wait patiently for my speech to end to drink her refilled glass.

"But…just because I'm also super excited for you! I think Rob is right. You and Jake are, of course, getting back together. And, like, soon."

"You think so?"

I could see her start to blush just considering the idea. It was clear those two loved each other; they just might drive us up a wall for the rest of our lives.

"Yes!" Robin and I shouted in unison.

"Okay, okay. Maybe. I will admit that it *was* good to see him. He had on this white shirt that buttoned down just to the middle of his chest, a black three-quarter-sleeve jacket over that, these khaki pants that showed off his ankles and were just tight enough to remind me what he's got going on under them, and some low-top red sneakers. He looked sooo good! Mmm."

"Ew. We don't want to hear that," I laughed.

"You're right. Sorry!" She ate another nacho to squelch her embarrassment, but I could see the dreamy twinkle in her eyes. My girl was in *love* love. It was inspiring to see. "Continue your toast!"

"Thank you." I lifted my chin high and finished my moment. "To y'all! The best, most inspiring, beautiful, bomb, loving friends a girl could ask for. You both deserve the world for real."

"Wait, wait! And to you, too," Robin interjected just as I was putting the rim of the glass to my lips. "Because I can't wait to see what this new job's going to be that you're dreaming up! All I know is what-ever it is, you're going to kill it."

"Mmm-hmm, she's right."

"Okay, then. To me, too! Because also after you two leave, I'm putting on some sexy shoes and going to U Street to go freak my man. Thanks for the inspi-

ration, Rae." I winked at her in the way that Robin
and Nick do so often when they are reassuring people, attempting to disarm them or giving them credit
for something they'd done.

"All right!!" Reagan raised up onto her knees on
the floor, lifting her drink into the air, too. "Now,
that's what I'm talking about!"

The three of us clinked our glasses and then guz-
zled down our drinks like we were back in college
and on a mission to get as drunk as possible.

"Whew! Brain freeze!" Robin screamed out upon
downing hers in one gulp.

"Well, kick that quickly. Because we still have to
talk outfits—"

"And it's 9:50 p.m., and our girl has somewhere
to be after," Reagan said, returning my wink from
earlier.

She wasn't wrong.

Officially tipsy—okay, maybe even a little drunk—
from our girls' night in, I downed the last of my sixth
glass of margarita as soon as Robin and Reagan said
their goodbyes. Then, inspired by the passion in Reagan's recounting of seeing Jake, I freshened up (my
mama called it a hoe bath growing up), changed into
some sexy lingerie and slipped on my Amina Muaddi
green satin sling-back Begum heels embellished with
a sparkling crystal brooch on the pointed toe. I was
going to get my man.

At the closet near my front door, I found my white

polka dot trench jacket that tied at my waist and flared out, the hem hitting just below my knees. It was the perfect thing to wear on an October night when you didn't want anyone but your boyfriend to see what you had on underneath.

Twelve minutes later, my Uber car was pulling up to Nick's place. I stepped out, thanked my driver and walked into the multilevel glass-and-brick building. By the time I was knocking on Nick's door, I was so excited with anticipation that my panties could barely hold in my juices. I had it all planned out. As soon as he opened the door, I'd unfasten my jacket and stand there letting him take me in from head to toe. Then, when he was ready to touch me, I'd step inside, walk just past him as I allowed my jacket to fall off me and drop down to my knees, revealing the black lace thong tucked in between my butt cheeks.

"Come here," I'd whisper.

And without a word, his lips would be on the back of my neck, then down my spine and finally on the fabric of the thong as he pulled them down over my hips with his teeth.

I couldn't wait.

But Nick's face didn't have the sparkle I envisioned in my fantasy when he saw me at his door.

"Hey," he said, rubbing his eyes. "Why didn't you use your key?"

"Well, I wanted you to greet me at the door," I answered, starting to undo the tie around my waist.

"That's weird, but okay."

Before I could say anything else, he turned back into the apartment and began walking to his living room.

"Wait, I meant I wanted you to see me at the door."

"Oh. My bad."

Nick spun around and watched me, his eyes glazing over, as I exposed myself and my black teddy to him.

"I was hoping you'd see this and—" My eyes pleaded with his not to embarrass me in the moment. I could see he was either tired or had been sleeping or both, but I hadn't come all this way, filled up with margarita confidence, just to be rejected by my boyfriend.

"You look beautiful, babe."

"Thanks, babe." I went to drop the jacket down my body like I'd fantasized, but then I heard him yawn. Loud and long like before.

"But can we not do this tonight? I'm exhausted."

"Can we not do this?!" I repeated his question back to him, flabbergasted. "Your girlfriend is standing in front of you practically naked, and you're acting like I just asked you to come with me to some fancy ball that you don't want to attend. Are you serious right now?"

I was heated. And embarrassed. And suddenly cold. I pulled the jacket back over me and tied it closed as tight as I could.

"Listen. I just said I'm exhausted. I had a hard day today—just got home about thirty minutes ago, and all I was looking forward to doing was crashing in my bed and sleeping until eleven tomorrow."

"I'm sorry I ruined such exciting plans," I mumbled under my breath but loud enough for him to hear.

"Don't do that," Nick said, growing upset as well. I could hear it in the way his normally nonchalant, deep voice suddenly rose an octave and became stern. "While you and your friends were drinking tequila all night, I was working. So, sorry, no, I'm not really interested in whatever replica fairy tale of Rebecca and Oliver or Reagan and Jake you have concocted tonight."

"Wait, what?!" Clearly, this was my phrase for the entire evening. I stood there with my mouth agape, listening to Nick's words, but completely confused. Replica? What was he talking about? "I'm not trying to replicate anything. I'm trying to make love to my boyfriend, who I love!"

"No. That's not it. For the past couple months, all you've done is compare us to your friends. You came here with those stupid-ass handcuffs the other day, and I indulged you because I'm like, 'maybe this is what she wants now.' Before then, you called yourself, trying to make me choose between you and some sexy lingerie and food that I clearly wanted, and now this. It's too much, Jenn. It's almost like all you think about is sex lately. I'm tired and over it."

"I thought you liked the handcuffs and…" I stopped myself before trying to address everything he'd just spouted out. Instead, I tried to step closer into his space to reconnect with him before things went too awry.

But as I stepped in closer, Nick backed up a few paces and continued talking.

"I mean, they were cool or whatever, but not necessarily me. And the more I think about it, the more I think you're trying to change me into your friends' men. And listen, I like them! But I'm not Oliver or Jake, and I don't want to be. Do you want them or me?"

"I want the man I was seeing six months ago."

"Well, he's tired and wants to go to bed."

"That's all you ever want to do. Literally. That's it. You don't see anything wrong with that?!"

"Because I work, Jenn! What do you want from me?"

"Nothing." I dropped my head and began walking back to his front door. I pulled my phone out my jacket pocket, flipped to my Uber app and began pricing to see whether Lyft or Uber would get me home faster and cheaper than the other. Either way, I just knew I needed to be out of his presence and ASAP.

"Wait, Jenn. I'm sorry." Nick followed me and put his hands on my shoulders, trying to get me to turn back to him. I could feel the tears in my eyes screaming to get out, however, and I really didn't want to give him the pleasure of seeing me cry.

"I'm not trying to be a jerk. I just… It's just a lot

going on right now. And you show up with this Rebecca kind of move, and don't get me wrong, it's sexy, but it doesn't feel like you. Can you just come upstairs, we'll cuddle…just be together, like old times? I love you. Please don't leave."

I stood there, my back still facing him, and listened to every hurtful word he said to me. *Doesn't feel like you. Like old times.* He really had no idea how much that stung. And I didn't have it in me to explain it, not tonight, not after all that had just happened.

"I think it's best I go home," I said after a few seconds of silence swept between us. "And my car is pulling up in one minute."

"Jenn."

"Bye, Nick."

I opened his door and walked into the hallway, my eyes focused on just getting to the elevator before I broke down. I never looked back at him, and he made no further attempts to stop me.

Chapter Twelve

The next morning, I woke up around 6:00 a.m., looked at my clock in disgust and rolled over to go back to sleep. A few minutes later, my phone alarm went off. With barely one eye open, I pressed dismiss and noticed my Saturday morning horror: Nick hadn't texted or called me since I left him last night.

I could have pretended it was all an awful dream, except right next to my bed were the green satin heels and black teddy as evidence. Vaguely, I recalled slipping out of both when I got home, throwing on a nightshirt and climbing into my bed—deep underneath my covers—and crying myself to sleep. Nick and I had never fought like that, not in the entire three years I'd known him. And yet, there were no missed calls or texts on my phone. No "I just want to know you made it home safely" messages. Nothing.

How was that even possible? I turned my phone over so that I could no longer see the screen and placed it on my nightstand. That was easier than staring at it in disbelief and replaying last night's events in my head. The way he just stood there and watched me leave sent a cold chill down my spine. One that only my duvet cover, plus my blanket, both wrapped around me like a swaddle, could seem to solve.

As the day grew older, the sun dared to peek through my curtains, but I had no intention of leaving my cover cocoon anytime soon. I squeezed one arm out, leaned all the way over to one side and grabbed the eye mask off my dresser. It would take more than a little sun to get me up, especially when I had backup. With my eyes now fully covered, I returned to my sweet spot in the bed and was sound asleep in less than two minutes.

It was 3:30 p.m. the next day when I finally forced myself to get up. And that only happened after fifteen minutes of torturous listening to my phone ping over and over from what was obviously a group text chain conversation that I had no interest in. I finally picked up my phone and saw the latest text from Reagan.

Oh, I found the cutest outfit for the party! I can't wait for y'all to see it.

Upon opening the notification, I saw that she'd jump-started the text chain between me, her and Robin while out running errands for our party. She'd apparently set her heart on either a big multilayer, wedding-style cake for us or a set of three comparatively smaller—but still way too fancy—cakes, so she was also stopping at a litany of DC bakeries and pricing out what options they had for both. I would have probably gone to Costco and bought some sheet cakes, but that's why she was in charge of the food and not me. I read through the recent messages between the two of them before deciding if I would participate.

Robin: Ugh, I can't believe we agreed not to tell each other what we were wearing. I want to know what you got!

Reagan: That's just because you're nosy and probably want to style me. But you're going to have to wait two more weeks like everyone else *winky face*

Robin: Grrr. 1 out of 10. Do not recommend friends who have 20K followers gawking over their #shoeoftheday Instagram posts. Suddenly, they think they don't need you!

Reagan: You'll be all right, Rob. I promise lol

Wait, Jenn, are you there?

Robin: Yeah, earth to Jenny.

Well, that callout meant that I couldn't keep ignoring their texts. I reluctantly, finally responded.

Yes?

Reagan: Are you all right over there?

Robin: Yeah, did you fall down a Nick rabbit hole after we left Friday night? We haven't heard from you since.

Me: Something like that, but not in a good way.

Reagan: Oh, no, what happened? Wait, let me step out of this bakery so we can video chat.

One thing about my friends—they were always ready when one of us said something was wrong. But I wasn't in any position to be on video. I hadn't even taken my head scarf off from the night before. Plus, I didn't want anyone to see my puffy, tear-streaked face.

I'm under my covers and don't want to move.

Reagan: Okay, so then we'll call.

For the next ten minutes, I spun the whole sad,

painstaking story for them, recalling the dismissive ways Nick told me he wasn't Oliver, the way he made a super feeble attempt to get me to stay after blasting me for what felt like an hour, and even my awful walk of shame back home from my Uber car. I left out the parts about Jake so that Rae wouldn't feel uncomfortable but made sure to home in on just how embarrassing it feels returning home with only a jacket covering up all your lady bits, a mascara-stained face and no sex to make you feel better.

"I'm sure I was my driver's wild story when he got home," I said, rounding the end of my tale. "I could hear it now. 'Babe, you'll never guess what happened today. This poor girl was practically naked in my car, but she looked like the world had fallen on her.' And he wouldn't have been wrong in his assessment."

"That's not the Nick we know and love. I'm so sorry, Jenn."

Robin, usually the one ready to bite a dude's head off for hurting one of her friends, was surprisingly calm in her response. She was also seated under a hot hair dryer at her favorite Dominican salon, so she was making every effort not to raise her voice in public while talking on her headphones.

"That's all you have to say? After I completely humiliated myself and…" I looked at my phone screen to verify what I was going to say before continuing. "Still, more than forty hours later, he's said nothing?!"

"Well, I—"

"What? Do you agree with him?"

"I absolutely do not agree with how he treated you and spoke to you. That's whack as hell. But...you did tell us that you haven't felt like yourself lately, so maybe he's just picking up on that and didn't know how to express it."

"Except that I've felt more like myself in the past couple weeks than I have in a while. I'm starting to get excited about work again now that I've been researching what I could do around behavior management and curriculum training. I feel sexy and alive again, and *that's* the person he claims not to recognize. That can't be a good sign for us."

"Sigh. Men," Reagan interjected. "Why have we been cursed to love them so much?!"

"Seriously."

"Okay, but listen," Robin said, jumping back in. "You're right. Friday night was straight *basura*. And I'm pissed that he hasn't called you since then. That's not okay. And I still know it's all going to work out. Both can be true, right? And when it does, don't you worry, I will appropriately knock him upside his head for being such a jerk."

"Mmm. I guess, Rob." I smiled just a bit, not realizing until then how much I'd needed to hear my friends pull for me and not just my relationship. "I like how you threw in a little Spanglish since you're at the salon, though."

"You know she can't help herself!"

"Hey, whatever. Somebody's gotta say what Chrissy would say, right?"

And there it was, our regular mention of Christine—always intended to honor her and make us feel like she was still connected with us—but usually just making us really sad. The silence wafted over the phone for another sixty seconds before Reagan finally spoke up.

"This is true," she said, a slight crack in her voice that gave away her secret—that she'd probably just stopped herself from crying. "Plus, Rob is right. Once Nick sees you at our party, he won't be able to resist that thang!"

"Uh."

"Uh, what?" Robin asked, still whispering but slightly louder than she probably intended.

"I kind of haven't gotten my outfit yet."

"Are you kidding me?" Robin straightened up in her seat, wincing equally from the heat on her scalp and from my disclosure. "Okay, no. It's time to get out of the bed right now and go shopping."

"I have my shoes, though! Rae, you'd be proud of that!"

"Nope, don't try to appeal to her. Get up."

"Well, I am proud of that. But she's right. You can sulk after you shop. Plus, retail therapy is best for this kind of thing."

"Sigh. Okay. I'm getting up now."

Silence.

"You know we can hear that you're not moving, right?" Reagan asked.

"Okay, okay!" I finally climbed out of bed and walked to my bathroom, switching on the lights and facing myself in the mirror. "I'm up and moving. Happy?"

"Yes," they said in unison.

"And let us know when you're out and shopping, too. I just might join you after I get this cake situation settled."

"Oh, no, you don't. You don't get to see her outfit when I couldn't see yours."

"I mean…"

"No, Jenn will do this on her own like everyone else. And we and her man are going to be gawking like she's Cinderella when we see it on her."

"If he comes," I reminded them.

"Please. He's coming. I'm not even entertaining that. All right, love you, gotta go. My hair dryer just finished, thank God. I thought my scalp was going to peel off if I had to spend five more minutes under this thing."

"Beauty is pain! I love you, too."

"Saaaame," Reagan screeched out before they both hung up their phones.

Alone again in my bathroom with my thoughts, I splashed water on my face and attempted to pull myself together. Nick might have thrown me for a loop, but they were right—I had stuff I needed to accomplish, with or without a man by my side.

Within an hour, my multicolor Vans (yellow, red, green and white, and they were hella cute, thank you very much!) and I were walking to the subway. But not to go shopping as Reagan and Robin suggested. Unlike my friends, who somehow managed to still find cute clothes in retail stores, I made most of my purchases online. So, I promised myself that I'd hop on my laptop to peruse Boohoo, ASOS, Amazon and others later that night. I even set an alarm just in case I needed that extra bit of motivation.

Instead of shopping, I decided to meet up with a coworker at Meridian Hill/Malcolm X Park to discuss the ideas I'd started putting together to present to my vice principal, Phillip, about a new job. While getting dressed, I realized that what I needed more than clothes for my birthday party was to focus my attention on my career. That was the biggest cause of my problems lately, and it needed to be resolved whether Nick and I got back together or not.

Felicia was a firecracker of a woman, five foot three, with the voice of someone six feet tall. She'd moved to DC after attending college in Atlanta and immediately started working as a teacher but found herself burned out by it ten years in. Much like me.

Unlike me, she didn't hesitate to do something about it. While still working, she obtained her master's degree in counseling with a concentration in career development. Then she started slowly infusing what she learned into her coursework, taking notes on its effectiveness at our school specifically and using this experience to get herself the job she really wanted. And at thirty-four, Felicia became our school's first career counselor—a rarity in elementary education. She was also the last person who'd convinced Phillip to think outside the box when she was ready to leave the classroom, so I knew she'd give it to me straight if anything I mentioned sounded like I was asking for too much.

Thankfully, she was free on a random Sunday afternoon. All I had to do was meet her at Meridian Hill Park, where, apparently, Felicia regularly spent her Sundays participating in and occasionally watching the weekly drum circle that featured everyone from yogis, hipsters, college students, hula-hoopers and casual strollers walking by who couldn't resist the syncopated sounds beaming throughout the twelve-acre park. This was what she did at almost thirty-seven years old with a six-month baby in her belly while it took me getting fussed at by my friends to crawl out of bed today.

Like I said, firecracker.

When I got to the park and looked at all the stairs I had to climb, I was glad I wore my sneakers. It was also still pretty warm for an October day in DC, with a high of seventy-five showing up on my weather app. But I didn't need my phone to tell me that; the sweat threatening to trickle down my forehead and the countless people sitting out in the park as if it were a summer day in July told me everything I needed to know.

"Hey, Jennifer, up here!" Felicia called out from the very top, as if I couldn't see her and that basketball she was carrying under her sundress. I could. I just needed to give myself a second.

"I see you! Hey, girl! I'm coming—it just might take me another fifteen minutes before I make it up there!"

"Oh, please. Not with that skinny body and those Michelle Obama arms. I don't believe you one bit."

"That's from yoga, not stair-step cardio," I said, laughing, but then had to stop again halfway up the steps to take in some breaths. My lungs made it very clear that I couldn't both laugh and climb at the same time.

I finally made my way to the top and felt like I was Rocky running the stairs at the Philadelphia Museum of Art. Except far less triumphant, and with much less grace. Felicia had no sympathy for me and immediately started walking to where she'd put her blanket down on the upper mall. But I felt like the drum circle—that, sure, took place every Sunday from 3:00 to 9:00 p.m.—was especially celebratory in response to my effort.

"C'mon, girl, it's like twenty steps. You don't need to be so dramatic."

"It's wayyy more than that. Don't do that!" I bent down and caught my breath again, scanning my eyes over all the people in the park to see if they were judging me. Thankfully, I wasn't even on their radar. "Okay, okay. I'm here!"

Surrounding us were hundreds of people of all different races and sizes, some dancing with the drum circle, others picnicking off to the side with their friends either on benches or various plots of grass. There was even a Frisbee game going on across the park, which seemed as if it was at least a mile away, and some bikers riding along the square pathway. I always knew the park was a vibrant scene on the weekends when the weather was nice but probably hadn't been since I was a student at Howard using it as our backyard. Once we sat down, I finally asked the burning question that had been in my head my whole walk up to her.

"How did you get your very pregnant self up all those steps?"

"Jennifer, I come here almost every Sunday," she said nonchalantly while pulling some grapes out of the container in her backpack. "It's just normal to me now."

"Oh. That makes sense, I guess."

"Don't worry, a lot more will make sense when we're done here." She slid over to me another container that contained fried chicken. "Eat. And tell me this plan you have in mind."

"Well, I don't have it fully fleshed out yet, but I started with a list of things that I've enjoyed doing the past eight years and ones I wanted to grow into. Then I researched education positions that included some of them."

"And what did you find?"

"The best one seemed to be a dean of students position."

"Ooh, I like the way that sounds. Tell me more." Her excitement was only contained by the food she was stuffing into her mouth. But she looked so cute doing it that I almost wanted to take a photo of her. *Man, talk about pregnancy privilege.* Although, I'm sure she probably thought the opposite.

"It seems to be a job where you get to mainly focus on developing plans and curriculum to improve how it is delivered to students. You also may handle discipline issues and do a lot of work around staff training and strategies to support student success."

"Mmm, okay, I like this so far."

"The problem is most deans of students have a master's in education, and I don't have that."

"But you have a degree in psychology, right?"

"And English."

"Damn, girl. Okay, star! So, you have a double degree, which means you're not opposed to work."

"I am definitely not opposed to work."

"So, then get the master's…and get Kendall to pay for it."

"You think they would go for it?"

"Absolutely. Because I'm going to tell you all about how I did."

"Please do. I'm all ears."

Felicia sat up straight and dropped the food she had in her hand, which told me she was getting serious.

"The first thing you're going to have to do is agree

to stay with them for at least a few years after you get your master's degree."

"I can do that," I said. "I don't want to leave Kendall. I just want to do more than what I'm doing now."

"Good, good. That's going to be big, because no one wants to pay for you to get something and then you just leave. Now, you're also going to have to convince Phillip that your work won't be affected by you taking on the extra responsibility of being a student again. I think your double-major background will help that."

"Yeah, that makes sense."

"And lastly, you have to remind him about all the amazing things you've done already just in your position as teacher and grade-level chair. This is not the time to be humble. List it out and make it clear that if he gives you the role you're asking for, it will only empower you to excel even more. You do all that and it's a shoo-in. He's not going to want to lose you."

"I hope you're right," I said sheepishly.

"Oh, I am. Trust me."

Behind us, I could hear the beat of the drums getting louder.

"Ooh," Felicia said, jumping up to her feet. "Let's take a quick dance break and come back to this. It'll feed your spirit and give you some confidence in those bones."

"Wait, but there's so much more to discuss," I whined.

"Trust me. You need this first."

Felicia pulled me up by arms, and we danced our way over to the drum circle, letting our bodies feel the rhythm of the beats and taking in the spirits of our ancestors to help us keep moving forward. We swung our hips and moved our limbs in a way that was equal parts energizing and sacred, mesmerizing and divine.

Thirty minutes later, we returned to Felicia's blanket and began plotting out exactly how I would get the job I wanted, from the school I wanted, red tape and school bureaucracy be damned.

Chapter Thirteen

"Tell me, what do you love most about Nick?"

Three days later, I was back in Diane's office for my second therapy session. Her office hadn't changed since the first time I was there. It was still the same surprisingly colorful space with the burnt orange sofa, tissues at the ready and Blackness permeating from the walls and bookshelf. But some parts of me had changed, for the better and maybe the worse.

In just two weeks' time, I'd become more excited about my job prospects, I was starting to feel less lonely and invisible around my friends, and I'd even thought, for a brief moment, that Nick and I were getting back on track. Sadly, I couldn't have been more wrong on the last front. So, even though my original plan for my second therapy session was to focus on all the progress I'd made, I couldn't get past the tear-soaked soap opera episode of the Jenny and Nick show to get to any of the other items. Which was especially sad, because I'd initially really hoped to talk to Diane about my dean of students idea.

After listening to me recall every detail of the last two weeks in the Nick saga—from the romantic dinner to the handcuffs to the blowup and then the fact that I still hadn't heard from him in five days—Diane sat back in her chair and waited for my response to her very simple, very short question.

"I love everything about him," I finally answered.

"Well, that can't be true. You've been trying to change him at least since we've met, probably much longer than that."

Wow, so that was what she meant the last time when she said she'd challenge me on my thinking. I couldn't lie—that stung, but she was probably accurate in her assessment. I sat up on the sofa and tried again.

"You're right. And that probably hasn't been fair. I guess I've just been trying to get us back to what we were when we first met."

"Three years ago, right?"

"Right."

"Do you really want your relationship to be the same as it was three years ago?"

"I guess not."

This time, Diane leaned in closer to me before speaking. I could see she'd picked up a pen and was twirling it in her hand even though her notebook was still sitting too far away from her to write anything down.

"Jenn, remember, I don't want you to tell me what you think I want to hear. Let's be honest. Do you want your relationship to be the same?"

"I don't, honestly. I love that we've grown with each other. That there are things we know about each other now that we don't even have to speak aloud. I love that I know his family and friends and talk to them even when he's not with me. I love that we're comfortable enough around each other that one long bear hug from him can be enough to calm down whatever frustrations I had earlier that day. But if I'm honest—"

I paused and sighed. "I do miss the lust and desire, and even the intimacy of us getting to know each other, which required us talking more about what was going on in our lives and how we felt about it. That's the part I want back."

"Okay, and you said you told him this during the dinner you planned, right?"

"Yes. And I don't think he liked hearing it, of course. But he said he understood. And then we made love that night like I've been aching for us to do for months. All for it to end less than a week later. It just doesn't make sense."

I threw my arms up in frustration. My tears had

turned to confusion and then anger as I continued to parse out my feelings.

"What about what he said to you about feeling as if you were comparing him to Oliver and Jake? What do you think about those statements?"

"Honestly, Diane, I think it's a load of crap. If he felt that way, and apparently it seems like he has for a while now, why not say something earlier? I've been asking him to talk to me, tell me how he's feeling, tell me what's going on at work—and all I get it is 'I'll do better, babe.' 'I don't want to dwell on work stuff when I'm with you.' But then you're obviously holding in all this resentment, and I don't know anything about it? How is that fair?! Plus, if he'd bothered asking me, I would have told him that I don't want him to be anything like Oliver or Jake. I want him to be Nick, but I want him to *want* me again. Is that so much to ask?"

"It is not."

"I think what hurts more than anything he said that night is that I still haven't heard from him. We've never gone five days without talking to each other, not since the day we first met, and now he's just okay with watching me leave and never talking to me again? After everything we've been through together? I was with him when they buried his grandma two years ago. He's been with me as I try to navigate what I want to do with my career. And that's just it? It feels cruel. It feels unworthy of the love we've shared."

"Do you think it's over, really?"

"It's been five days. What would you think?"

"I would think maybe he needed some time to process all of the feelings you said he doesn't normally express. It sounds to me like those all came pouring out of him—and I don't know him, so I won't make a diagnosis—but I'd be willing to bet that he probably feels a lot of shame for how he reacted."

"Maybe. Toni Braxton said seven whole days and not a word from you, seven whole days and I'm just about through…so, you know, he's got two more days."

Diane wrapped her hands over her mouth as she tried to hold back her giggles, which caused me to chuckle, too. That chuckle then built into a loud, roaring laughter that neither she nor I could contain. In a weird way, it was just what I needed to break up the anger/sadness/confusion cycle I'd been in for days. It was probably the first time I'd laughed long and hard since Friday, too.

"I don't think you should be taking advice from '90s R&B music," Diane finally said after she was able to compose herself somewhat.

"Well, why not? Everyone always says, 'If it's not '90s R&B love, I don't want it.'"

"Yeah, and I never understood that meme or phrase, because '90s R&B music is littered with the side chick calling the woman to tell her that her man has been cheating, men begging and falsely claiming that they can perform sexual acts for ten-plus hours—until the sun comes up, my ass, only if we started at 5:55 a.m.—and even more women just outright saying how much they could love someone else's man better than them. People are looking back at these songs with rose-colored glasses."

"OMG, you're so right. I love them, but SWV's whole catalog of singles, outside of 'Right Here,' was about being the other woman."

"Exactly. That might be a slight exaggeration, but essentially, it's true! So, I'm not saying that Toni is wrong or that your man not calling you in seven days isn't trash, but I have questions. Did she call him at all in those seven days? Matter of fact, have you called Nick?"

"No," I said, hanging my head in shame. "But that's because I shouldn't have to. He saw me leave his apartment in tears in the middle of the night, and he hasn't so much as checked on me to see if I'm alive. That's awful."

"You're right. But two things. A) Have you posted on social media since you left his apartment? And b) are you more concerned with being right or with working together to fix what's wrong in your relationship?"

"I've posted," I said quietly.

"Okay, so I'm assuming he follows you, since he's your boyfriend. So, it's safe to assume that he knows you're alive. Now, what about the next question?"

"Can't I want both?"

"Sure, you can absolutely *want* both. But the reality is you might not be able to get both right now. And I'm not saying that you need to call him and apologize or anything like that. How he handled what he was feeling was inappropriate, and you should feel like you can tell him that. But this silent treatment that you are *both* giving? It's not getting you any closer to what you want—a fulfilled life with this man."

"Sigh. You're right, Diane. You're right."

"So, what do you want to do now?"

"I guess I'm going to reach out to him and see if we can talk about what happened."

"Okay, but only if that's truly what you want to do. Is it?"

"Yeah, it is," I said, slightly more confident in response the second time.

"Do you want to take the last ten minutes to talk through some ways to make sure you don't end up taking on the sole blame for what has gone wrong and that you are able to express your hurt in a clear manner?"

"I would really love that, Diane. Thanks."

Later that night, I lay in my bed and repeatedly listened to Teyana Taylor's "Issues/Hold On" through the Spotify app on my phone. Diane had given me a lot to think about during our session, and I was determined not to let my ego end my relationship. After the sixth time of hearing Teyana wail about how much she was fighting to keep her relationship together while hoping it was worth the try, I finally psyched myself up enough to call Nick. I sat up and, with all the hope that I could muster, too, clicked his name on my phone and waited with bated breath for him to answer.

After the fourth ring, I realized that he wasn't going to. Devastated, I hung up the phone, wondering if we really were over without either of us having even tried to fight for the other.

Just as I was about to climb under my duvet cover, I heard a familiar ping from my phone, signaling that I received a text message. I wasn't in the mood to talk to anyone, but I picked it up anyway to see who it was from.

It was Nick.

Hey, Jenn, saw you called. I'm sorry I haven't.
You deserve better than that.
You deserve better than me.
But I just can't talk about it right now.
I hope you're okay.

I stared at my phone like it was a message telling me that I'd been shot. It didn't seem real, because I would have felt it, right? That was what Nick had effectively done to me—he shot me Friday night and was now just telling me about it later. I wasn't sure what I could possibly say in response to his texts. Diane and I had talked about me not taking on the full blame in an effort to reassure him of my love, so I didn't want to do that. And I was angry that he put me in the awkward position of having to comfort him over text because he'd said he didn't deserve me, when he could have just picked up the phone when I called so that we could talk about what happened like adults.

In fact, the more I stared at my phone, the angrier I got as my tears pierced through my eyes. Here I was, sucking up my pride so that I could fight for us, and he just…hoped that I was okay? In what world did he think that was good enough? To top it all off, he also didn't text that he loved me. At the very least, if he did that, I could have simply texted back that I loved him, too, and that I wanted us to work things out. Now, I was more scared than ever that we wouldn't. With little energy left to spend on him, I finally texted back.

Hope you're okay, too. We should talk soon.

After pressing Send, I silenced my phone and turned my music back on, but this time not back to Teyana. No, I needed Jazmine Sullivan to get me through my new mood. As the guitar from "Girl Like Me" began to play, I lay back down and let her sing me to sleep.

Part 3

"A flower does not think of competing to the flower next to it, it just blooms."

—Zen Shin

Chapter Fourteen

Being one of the three guests of honor for the Reagan, Jennifer and Robin Thirtieth Birthday Bash felt sort of surreal until the day finally came. Up until then, so much effort had gone into what we would do and wear and say, whom we'd invite, when we'd walk in, and what food and drinks we'd have that I'd started to feel a little removed from whatever magical moment I'd initially hoped I'd feel when I walked in.

Compounded on that was the reality that two weeks had gone by and Nick and I were no closer to resolving our issues; we hadn't even talked since he texted me that I deserved better than him. So, to be honest, despite all the effort we'd put in, I wasn't expecting much. More than anything, I was praying that I'd get through the night unscathed and end up just the right amount of drunk that I could look back on the evening, remember it fondly and still have the occasional friend tell me about something that I didn't remember happened.

So, color me surprised, because when I stepped into Harlot DC and looked around at the pink, purple, champagne and gold decor; the flowers that draped across the ceiling, the walls and even the bar; the chandeliers and candles that lit up the place but also caused a distinct type of mood setting that instantly made you feel like a boss-ass woman, I did indeed have a moment when my breath was taken away. Suddenly, all that we'd planned, all the little intricacies we included, the ways we made sure to honor each of us and Christine with subtle nods to things we loved—it was all here and real and for us.

In one part of the lounge, the hot-pink spiral stairs, which inspired photo shoots from several of our friends, were surrounded by some of Reagan's favorite heels. The bar featured signs highlighting the signature cocktail that Robin loved to make whenever we weren't chugging down margaritas, whiskey gingers or tequila sodas—a pomegranate and orange prosecco punch topped with pomegranate seeds and mint leaves. The waiters were walking around with passed hors d'oeuvres of mini shrimp po' boys, crispy house-made fried dumplings and black bean fritter tacos—the likes of which Christine's mouth would have been drooling over for hours. And throughout the room, on every table and bar that had space, were images from some of my students' artwork in sparkly gold five-by-seven-inch picture frames.

It was a lot to take in at once, but it was so incredibly beautiful and uniquely us that, for just a minute, I almost shed a tear when the DJ announced us. Making our grand entrance fifty minutes after the party's stated start time (of course, a Robin idea), the three of us strolled in, in lock step together, hands intertwined, and set our eyes on the two hundred–plus friends and family that had come to celebrate with us. It was Howard's homecoming, after all, so many of them had several other party options they could have chosen; instead, they were here, dressed in their best suits and cocktail dresses, showering us with love.

"Ladies and gentlemen, the time has finally come," said DJ Jackie into her microphone, subtly turning down the music so she could be heard over it. "Please welcome your favorites, your family, the thirty and…well, almost thirty-year-old wonders, Reagaaannnn, Jenniferrrrr and Robinnnnn."

We hadn't actually planned on the DJ sounding like an announcer at a basketball game, but somehow it worked. Just as she called out our names, the doors to the lounge swung open and the sound system began blasting Lizzo's "Like a Girl" as streamers of confetti blew into the air, plastering everything in sight. This included us and the outfits we'd spent hours putting together: Robin in her strapless black leather minidress and her Azalea Wang "Love Me Till It Hurts" studded stiletto pumps that tied partially up her calves; Reagan in a disco-blue V-neck dress that cinched at her waist and flared out, paired with light pink, ankle-strap sandals that just so happened to be Christian Louboutins; and me in a slinky, sequined, emerald-green off-the-shoulder dress that fell to midi length with a split up my right thigh, combined with my new nude crystal-strapped pointed-toe Jimmy Choo heels.

Just to put an exclamation point on the entrance, someone slapped each of our immaculately press-on–nailed hands around glasses of the signature cocktail, and before we knew it, twenty-five of our best girl friends were surrounding us, jumping up and down in their bejeweled dresses and heels, shouting the lyrics to Lizzo's song to no one and everyone all at once.

It was, in a word, infectious. And all ours.

"Happy birthday, ladies," DJ Jackie shouted over a combination of the music and singing. "We are so happy to be here to celebrate you tonight. I see you have your drinks. You're looking good. But the thing is…" She paused for dramatic effect. "You can't do birthdays without cake!"

As soon as she finished her statement, she dropped the beat to Rihanna's "Birthday Cake," and out of the corner of my right eye, I saw a seven-tier pink, purple, white and gold birthday cake topped with a gold sign that said "Dirty Thirty" in cursive. Each tier had its own chance to shine. The bottom was covered in hot-pink edible flowers. The tier right on top of it was a paler pink with a huge bow and swoops of fondant icing. Sitting on top of that was a dark purple tier with crisscross stenciling that made it look 3-D. Next was a lavender tier with gold accoutrements that were designed to look like charm bracelets with various pendants representing our hometowns—a fleur-de-lis for Reagan, the Golden Gate Bridge for me and a deep-dish pizza slice for Robin.

The fifth tier was the same pale pink as the second-to-last tier, but this time was covered in edible flowers. On top of that was a pure gold tier, which featured a white circle in the middle and "30" written in it in the same color gold as the cake. And to top off the extravagance, the last and seventh tier was bone white with what looked to be individually placed crystals all around it, with the topper sitting dead center on it.

Served us right for letting Reagan choose the cake. This thing, immaculately sitting on top of its custom-cake table, was taller than me! And maybe more expensive than anything I had on. But oddly enough, situated among everything else going on, the cake fit right in; I just had no clue how we were going to cut it.

"This is wild," I screamed while grabbing Reagan's hand. "What are we supposed to do with this thing?!"

"Whatever we want!" she shouted back, grab-

bing Robin's hand, too, and pulled us both toward
it. Thankfully, we'd only had a few drinks so far, because the heels we were wearing were barely made
for standing, much less for protecting us from falling while being dragged the thirty feet to the cake.
With the spotlight still on us, Reagan directed our
eyes to it and attempted to zero our focus in on just
the three of us instead of our surroundings.

"Ladies, tonight is *our* night. And we are going
to have a blast! Okay?!"

"Yesss!" Robin shouted back. "But does this mean
we have to eat this whole damn cake?"

Okay, maybe I was wrong, and Robin had had
more to drink during our pregame before our entrance to the party than I realized. It was the only
explanation for why she thought we were expected to
eat the whole cake, but her very real question drew
out the best kind of laughter from both me and Reagan. In fact, it was just what we needed to center
us among the chaos of the evening, even if Robin
couldn't yet comprehend why we thought her question was so funny.

"I'm just happy to be with you beautiful, amazing ladies," I said, with little tears in the corners of
my eyes.

"I am, too, but we're not crying tonight! At least
not yet." And with that, Reagan dropped our hands
and took hold of the gold knife lying on the cake
stand, picked a spot on the bottom tier of the cake
and officially made the first slice.

"Ayyyeeeeeeee," the crowd roared right as she pulled out the knife with the first slice cut. I guess they were all either very ready for cake or drunk or a bit of both. Either way, Reagan was focused on nothing but devouring her slice, so much so that she didn't blink an eye at the thought of the whole party watching her eat. She also barely noticed when Robin started jumping for glee. I did, however.

"Rob, babe. What's happening right now?" I asked cautiously.

"Oh, nothing," she said slyly. "Just that I noticed Jake in the freaking corner of the lounge!" Thankfully, the music was blasting so loud that I was pretty sure no one else could actually hear anything we were saying, but we heard her loud and clear. And that finally got Reagan's attention.

"Wait, he's here?"

"Yes, yes, this is what I'm saying!"

"Where?" Reagan scanned the entire lounge, trying frantically to find him but also not let on to the crowd that she was looking for someone. When she found him, however, it was pretty obvious. Anyone still focused on us after all this time saw her eyes and smile light up like a ten-thousand-watt bulb as soon as she spotted him.

"I can't believe he really came," she said wistfully.

"I told you he would."

"You did, and I didn't believe you."

"One day you two will finally listen to me."

"You hear this, Jenn? She's right about one little

thing and now she's the freakin' Dalai Lama and we've been ignoring her sage wisdom all this time."

"Oh, I hear her drunk tail, yes!" I laughed. "But to be fair, she was also right about Jake earlier this year when she predicted you two would get back together after our trip to Paris."

"Whatever, she's not Cleo!"

"Call me now," Robin immediately screamed out, mimicking the classic line by the infamous Black American television personality from the '90s who claimed she was a Jamaican shaman who could give you a tarot reading over the phone.

"Okay, byeeeeeeee, Robin! You are too much right now." I couldn't hold in my laughter if I tried, but my dress wasn't built for gut-busting giggles, so I needed her to stop being such a funny drunk.

"Don't dismiss me. You know I'm always right when it comes to these things."

"Well, I don't see Nick here tonight, so you're one out of two right now," I reminded her.

"I'm not worried at all. He'll be here before the night is over. I promise you that," Robin said matter-of-factly, flipping her bob as she tossed me her signature wink. "And in the meantime—and this is coming from the one person in this trio who won't have a man in her bed tonight, so indulge me—we are going to enjoy this moment, eat all this damn cake and celebrate the fact that we are thirty, we are fabulous and we are lit AF!"

"I'm here for that!"

"Me, too!" I said, just as someone slid another drink in my empty hand. I was a little worried that Robin still seemed intent on eating the whole cake, but who was I to ruin her fun? "You know what? Let's eat some cake!" I yelled out, this time loud enough for everyone else to hear.

"Ayeeeeeeee," responded the crowd again. And within seconds, they surrounded us with plates in their hands.

A couple hours later, after several strolls around the lounge to mingle with our friends and family and far too many signature cocktails that were slipped into my hands just as I finished the last one, DJ Jackie called us back to the middle of the room with every Black person's favorite version of the birthday song—Stevie Wonder's.

"All right, ladies, I know y'all have had beaucoup drinks tonight," she yelled into the mic after Stevie finished singing the chorus the first time. Her slightly Southern drawl might have given her away, but that *y'all* and *beaucoup* told anyone listening she was from New Orleans. In fact, she was Christine's cousin—yet another way we'd found to honor our friend during our celebration. It didn't hurt that she gave us the friends-and-family discount, too. "But it's time to come on back out here!"

Carefully, we each strolled back to the center of the room, until we were once again holding hands and basking in the glow of everyone singing the last parts of the song to us. I took a quick moment to close my eyes so that I could hear the joy all around us, still holding tight to my girls as we joined in singing, too. The night really was almost perfect; the only thing that could have made it better was Nick by my side. But the more I took in the love, the more I realized that even without Nick, our party had turned out to be everything we wanted and more. And I was happy—genuinely, ridiculously, uninhibitedly happy.

Right as the song ended, and DJ Jackie began expertly mixing in Drake's "Ratchet Happy Birthday," I reopened my eyes and saw the only thing that could have possibly made my night better— Nick, standing on the purple wall, his eyes completely focused on me, even as he was talking to Rebecca. He'd come after all. After everything we'd been through, he showed up. And he looked damn good, standing there in an all-black suit: meticulously tailored black pants, a single-breasted black blazer and a black button-down shirt that was undone three buttons down, giving a slight peek at his ankh tattoo. I had no clue what they were talking about, but whatever it was, it only had a piece of his attention. The sole reason I knew he was even sort of part of the conversation was because he was indeed talking back to her (I saw his mouth moving, at least!), but the whole time, his eyes—intense and steady and filled with lust—were on me.

And that had me in a strange hold where I couldn't tear my eyes away from his. In the middle of all the

chaos and the glitter and glam and birthday songs, I
was his to control from all the way across the room.
It wasn't until I saw Rebecca quickly bolt away from
him that I sort of started to snap back to reality. But
then I smiled, and he smiled back, and the crowded
room fell away again. I'd completely forgotten I was
in the center of the lounge—until I heard Reagan
calling my name…into a microphone, no less. What
had I missed?

The next thing I knew, Rebecca was coming from
the left side of the room, bouncing toward us in her
black-and-teal sandals that zipped up her ankles, carrying two extra-large, matte black gift bags. And
she was headed toward Reagan, who still held the
microphone.

"Well, Rob and Jenn, y'all already know how
much I adore the both of you," Reagan said into the
mic. The crowd awwed instantly, as I still tried to figure out what was going on. I wondered if Robin was
any clearer on the details, but then remembered she'd
started off the night tipsy, so she probably wouldn't
be much help. Rebecca, meanwhile, now stood directly beside Reagan, her face beaming—presumably
because of whatever was in the bags. "Well, one of
the most meaningful things you two have ever done
for me came inside a bag similar to this."

She turned to the crowd to acknowledge them
briefly. "Now, some of y'all might know this story,
but I'm going to tell it anyway. You see, the last
year has been really hard on us. You know that we

lost the best person I have ever known, Christine Vasquez. And I have to say, it's quite a feat that we are standing here today not utterly broken apart by her passing."

Reagan took a deep breath before she continued. The room had gone completely silent as she spoke about Christine, probably because most of the people there missed her just as much as we did. I knew that simple breath was Reagan's way of pulling herself back from the brink of tears so that she could get through whatever she wanted to say before she started crying. And so, I quietly egged her on, while also trying not to cry. "You can do it," I mouthed, and she started speaking again.

"But life wasn't a crystal stair even before Chrissy passed. At least not for me. I was struggling, spending all my time trying to perpetuate what I thought was a perfect life until I couldn't fake it anymore. And one day, I, the woman who adds 'rest' to her to-do lists because she plans out everything, up and quit my job. I knew it was the right decision, but once I got home and started thinking about *allll* the consequences of quitting your job out of nowhere, I was *thiiis* close to calling my boss back and being like, 'pleeeease take me back, I'm sorry!'"

Reagan punctuated her story with a slap on her thigh, having somehow done the impossible—turned the quiet, somber crowd back into a group of people laughing. It was amazing to see the energy shift, but I was still holding back tears, so I needed her to finish soon.

"And then these ladies showed up to my apartment, Rob, Jenn, Becs and Chrissy…carrying with them bottles of champagne and an extra-large gift bag that held a pair of designer heels that I'd bookmarked for when I had the courage to move on to a better job for me. In my eyes, I didn't deserve those shoes, because that's not what I'd done. But to them? They saw something brave in me that I didn't see at the time. The same way I see courage, and fierceness, and badassery in them right now. So, Rob. Jenn. In these bags are my birthday gifts to you—your own designer reward shoes, and a notebook and pen to maybe even start your own shoe-diary journey."

With her speech finally ended, Reagan walked toward us, giving us both our bags, our mouths fully open with a mixture of excitement, awe and speechlessness at Reagan's latest surprise. Who knew she had something up her sleeve even greater than the cake?!

"Reagan, I—"

"Don't fight it, Jenn. Just take the bag," she said, shoving it into my body.

With my directions made clear, I opened the gift bag and saw just what she had described: a beautiful blue notebook with a ballpoint pen attached to it, and a signature tan Christian Louboutin box. I passed someone closest to me my drink so that I could pull the box out of the bag and laid my eyes on the most gorgeous pair of shoes I'd ever seen. Inside the box was also a note from Reagan.

> *Jennifer, these are Christian Louboutin black studded PVC and suede Bille et Boule bow pointed-toe pumps. I know that means nothing to you, but that's what they are! Lol...more importantly, I want them to be a reminder to you that every woman needs a pair of shoes that helps her stand up tall on the days it's hardest, and that there's nothing wrong with a little spice in your life as long as it's what you want and brings you closer to learning yourself. Love, Rae*

That was it—I couldn't hold my tears in any longer. And really, I was known as the sensitive one in the group anyway, so it shouldn't have been a shock to anyone that I would cry at such a heartwarming gift. I turned to Reagan and threw myself on her, hugging her as tight as I could.

"I love your over-the-top self so much," I whispered in her ear. "Never change, okay?!"

"As long as you promise to keep doing whatever the hell you want to do and let whoever else step up to the plate or move on—including Nick—it's a deal!"

"Deal!"

To our right, Robin finished opening her box as well and jumped right into our sister-friend hug.

"Um, no way this is happening without me," she said, grabbing us both tight.

"Never!" I responded back through a tear-streaked smile.

"Okay, new pact," Robin said, our group embrace still going.

"Oh, no, not another pact. You two and this date pact have been enough."

"No, no, nothing like that. This is a pact for us. We vow that no matter where we go or who we end up with, this friendship is built to last."

"Now, that's a pact I can get behind," I replied, smiling.

"Me, too," said Reagan.

"Heyy, we want to see those shoes!" DJ Jackie yelled into the microphone, bringing us back to reality.

"Yesss," responded Reagan, jumping out of our sister circle and springing into action. "How could we ever forget the shoes?! Rob, you want to show yours first?"

"Well," Robin said lifting hers high in the sky. "According to Reagan, these are Sophia Webster Evangeline angel wing sandals, but let me tell you, all I see right now is this gold stiletto heel?! And these literal gold wings on the back of the black ankle strap, and I'm just going to say it—Sophia can call them what she wants. I'm calling them warrior sandals, and I am here for it."

"Yessss! Okay, Xena the Warrior Princess! And

we are here. For. You," DJ Jackie proclaimed over the mic. Her exuberance inspired even more shouts from our friends and family and calls for celebration.

Someone in the crowd, maybe it was Rebecca, screamed out, "Strike a warrior pose, Rob!" And upon hearing the request, Robin drunkenly tried to oblige, spreading her legs as far as she could with a minidress on, lifting her arms up and winking to the crowd.

It was certainly a sight to see.

After all our girlfriends sized up the shoes, telling us where we should wear them and when, DJ Jackie concluded the gift-giving portion of the evening with something that ended up being my best opportunity to sneak away to try to find Nick. As soon as she dropped Da Entourage's "Bunny Hop," it looked like all two hundred–plus people jumped into formation to line dance to the still-catchy tune from 2003.

While they danced, I started making my way to the bar, figuring it would give me a chance to sit while I scanned the room, hoping Nick hadn't come and then disappeared before we could even speak. To my pleasant surprise, I'd barely taken a few steps when I saw him standing right in front of me, with that same intense and sexy-as-hell stare from earlier.

"Hey," he said.

"Hey."

"It's been a while."

"Uh, yeah. Longer than I ever want it to be again."

"Me, too, actually. What do you say we step outside for a second so we can talk some more? Away from all the madness." Nick ended his sentence with a laugh, but I could tell it was more of a nervous chuckle than that he thought something was funny. Somehow, after all this time, it still seemed like he didn't know that I was all in for him. Like he was worried I might actually say no.

"I'd like that," I said and took his hand in mine as we walked outside, where, suddenly, we could hear ourselves speak without having to shout over music and other people screaming.

Chapter Fifteen

Harlot DC was conveniently located on the corner of Eleventh and U Streets NW, just a few blocks from Nick's apartment. While U Street was usually lively on a Saturday night, filled with people walking from bar to bar, the Eleventh Street side of the corner was much quieter. Indeed, immediately to the right of Harlot were simply a parking lot and a tree-lined row of houses—the perfect pocket of space for a couple that wanted to step outside a party for a moment but not completely leave it to, say, go back to the guy's apartment.

This was how Nick and I ended up in that very pocket, just a few feet away from the lounge entrance. Standing inches apart from each other, with my hands in his.

"Jenn, I have to apologize for…everything," he said, his eyes burning into mine. "I was an idiot for turning you away that night, and I've let my pride keep me from showing up at your door and groveling for your forgiveness every day since."

"Nick—" I said, not knowing if I should pull back from him, draw closer to him, immediately forgive him, make him grovel or what. I just knew it was good to see him again and I liked his hands enveloping mine.

"No, let me finish," he said, interrupting me. "I don't want you to reassure me out of this feeling. I want to own it and be honest with you."

"Okay." I settled into a comfortable stance, appreciating his effort and trying to calm down my own thinking. "I'm listening."

"The thing is, you were right. Something has been off between us. We both knew it, but you were willing to be honest about it. Of course, we love each other, but we lost the spark…got too comfortable."

"Yeah, we did."

"And I know it's everything you said before, but I gotta be honest, I hated hearing it. I tried to play it cool, but it just really felt like you were telling me that I wasn't enough. That our relationship didn't live up to some fairy tale of your friends' relationships. But instead of saying that to you, I let my ego take hold and just shut down. That's why I got so upset that night. I mean, yeah, I was tired, but I also felt like it was just another instance of you trying to tell me you needed someone more sexually spontaneous, like an Oliver, or more expressive, like Jake, and that pissed me off, because I love sex! And especially with you! I just…"

"Nick—" I tried to stop him again, wanting to explain that it was less about the sex and more about just wanting us to connect intimately again. I'd learned this through therapy since our fight, but I hadn't been able to say it to him yet—that, yes, I wanted to know he lusted after me, but even more than that, I missed the closeness we had when we shared our deepest thoughts with each other.

"No, I know that's not what you were doing now. I—I actually talked to Rebecca." He paused for a moment and shyly looked off to the side. "She helped me see the light."

"Tonight? Is that what you two were talking about earlier?"

"Nah, I talked to her the day after you left my place, actually. And then probably two or three times since then. When you saw us talking earlier, it was just her bigging me up for showing up."

"You did show up," I said, a small smile forming on my face.

"I had to. I couldn't let you keep thinking that I didn't love you or still want to be with you or whatever your beautiful, sensitive mind was probably thinking these past two weeks. And my bad on that, too. I know that was hurtful, but I just needed to make sure when I stepped back to you, I was ready." Nick pulled me closer to him, only slightly, but near enough that I could start to pick up the scent of his cologne.

"Ready for what?" I asked.

"To be vulnerable, to be real with you, to lay it all on the line…"

"And that's what you learned from Rebecca?"

"No, that's what I learned from finally listening to you. Once I got out of my own head, you know. I thought back to all the times you tried to connect with me and couldn't. And I realized how lonely that must have been for you. She just told me that my fears that you wanted someone else were unfounded, that, really, you just wanted what any woman wants—to be reminded that her man desires her, physically, mentally, spiritually…the whole nine."

"That's very true. Maybe I didn't do a great job of saying it."

"No, you did. You told me. I just wasn't listening, babe. And I'm sorry."

"Thank you," I said, leaning my body into his, desperately wanting to find my support beam again and melt into his embrace. I stopped myself from fully connecting our bodies, however. Not because I didn't believe he was sorry, but sorry didn't make up for abandoning me for two weeks. "It has been really hard without you these past couple weeks," I said. "And I love that you're here now and talking about your feelings. But you really hurt me. I thought we were over."

"I know."

"I deserved better than that."

"You did."

"So, what now?"

"Now? I guess that's up to you, really, Jenn. I want you back, and I'm willing to do whatever to make that happen."

"Whatever?" I asked, a sly smile forming on my face as I closed in farther on his personal space. It was killing me being that close to him and not sinking into the nook of his armpit and side torso that was practically made for me.

"For real. I'm yours, Jenn. Wholly and completely."

With those magic words, I let my guard down with Nick again. The truth was that I wanted to love him, and I missed him, and if he was finally willing to fight for us, then I was, too. I slid my hands out of his and removed the last bit of space between us, placing my head on his chest and my left arm around his body. This was where I was meant to be, where I wanted to be, and I couldn't fight it anymore.

"I also want to show you how much I crave every little thing about you," Nick said as he moved his hands to the small of my back and cupped me closer to him.

"Oh, yeah? Tell me more."

"What about if I show you while I tell you?"

"Mmm, okay."

I wasn't exactly sure what that meant but soon found out. In one swoop, Nick lifted me up, pouring light kisses onto my lips while he walked us even farther away from the bustling side of U Street and over to a stoop where he could sit me down. The high slit on the right thigh of my dress gave way as he carried me with my legs wrapped around his waist, giving his hands easy access to slip under the dress and knead my butt as we kissed. Once seated, he bent down in front of me and began pointing out with his tongue each inch of my body that he desired.

"This earlobe right here is my favorite," he said, licking his way from my cheek to my right ear and then down my neck. "It's just so suckable."

"And this collarbone, the way it dips right here?" Nick kissed the slope in my collarbone before continuing. "It makes me want to take you home right now! Thank God you wore this dress tonight."

I hadn't even thought about this part of my body being exposed as one of the highlights of my dress that evening, but I was instantly glad I wore it, too. As a plus, Nick had such great access to glide his tongue over the many parts of my figure because of the structure of the dress. Down he moved, over my breasts and torso, toward my thighs, and at each body part, he took great care to point out what he liked as he caressed or licked or kissed every portion of it. At the opening of the slit in my dress, he slipped his hand underneath again, using his fingers to maneuver around my thong, and easily entering my already wet and hungry vagina.

"Nick—" I cried out as he flicked his finger upward inside me, hitting my G spot and sending power waves through my body. Every cell in me wanted him right then and there, despite us being outside within earshot of hundreds of people—or maybe because of it.

"Yes?"

"I want you. Now." Literal goose bumps crawled up my skin when he slipped another finger inside me, leaving me almost breathless as I squirmed and struggled not to lose control and scream so loud that we'd wake the neighbors up.

"Good."

He must have sensed that I was on the brink of my orgasm, because the next thing I knew, he scooped me up from the stoop, placed himself where I was originally and positioned me so that I was once again straddling his thighs. I let my legs fall on each side of his—the split really coming in handier than I'd expected it to—and with a quick unzip of his pants, I allowed him to enter me and felt him grow inside me as I sat down deeper into his lap. Nick pulled me closer to him, and I wrapped my arms around him tightly as we rode a surge of pleasure that stemmed from my toes and went all the way to my eye sockets.

It was the most intimate, lustful sex we'd had in a long time. And it didn't take me coercing him or trying to seduce him. It didn't involve fake handcuffs or lace teddies. He'd wanted me all on his own. Not wanting to lose the moment, I held Nick tightly as the waves crashed down my body, and I fell limp on his. I was in heaven and would have almost forgotten we were still right outside the party if I didn't see Reagan and Jake running out of the building together just as Nick and I came—another set of lovebirds apparently rekindling their flame.

The next morning, I awoke in Nick's bed, happy as a clam in high water. He was still sleeping as I squirmed out of his big-spoon embrace, giving me ample time to turn toward him and admire the man in front of me. Watching him breathe, his chest rising and falling, I lay there and recalled how much fun we had the night before. After we went back inside, I was pretty sure we danced for another two hours before DJ Jackie started playing a New Orleans Second Line version of LeVert's "Casanova." Popularized by the Rebirth Brass Band, this version of the song was much raunchier than the 1980s cult classic original, but it was what many New Orleans parties used as their final hurrah.

And so did we. Reagan, Robin and I had our custom-made parasols swinging in the air while our guests flicked their wrists to the beats with the handkerchiefs we gave out as party favors. And Nick was by my side the whole time, singing, dancing, hugging on me and generally doing exactly what he said he would do—showing me just how much he wanted to be with me, mentally, physically and spiritually.

By the end of the night, we walked our tired selves back to his apartment, kicked off our shoes, tore off our clothes and crashed in bed within two minutes of arriving. I didn't even remember to wrap up my hair or wash off all the makeup I had on, but that was probably more because of all the signature cocktails I drank than it was due to exhaustion. Still, with all that occurring just a few hours before, Nick looked like he was the male version of Sleeping Beauty, resting without a care in the world, just waiting for someone to kiss him out of his slumber.

"Woman, I've told you about staring at me while I sleep," he said while opening one eye, his voice barely louder than a whisper.

"Sorry! It's just… I don't know, calming."

"You know what's calming to me?"

"What's that?"

"You. Over here in my arms."

He grabbed me and pulled me into him where my right arm covered his chest and my leg curved on top of his thigh. Then he closed his big arms around me, fully wrapping me up in him.

"See? This is much better."

In this position, I could hear his heart beating through his chest, and our breaths began to sync up, his chest falling as mine rose. It was the perfect symbol of a complementary partnership.

"You may be right."

"Mmm-hmm. You know I am. No need to say maybe." Nick closed his eyes and took in another deep breath, briefly jolting us out of sync. Thankfully, we quickly went back, like our bodies couldn't stand to be disassociated and automatically found their way back to the synchronicity. "It's Sunday, right? So, what do you have planned today?"

"Well, now that I'm here, I want to stay in this very same spot all day long. But honestly, I need to do some more research to prepare for my pitch to Phillip on Thursday."

"Damn, he agreed to it?" I could hear a tinge of sadness in Nick's voice mixed with his excitement. I wondered if it was because this was a reminder of all that he'd missed not being in my life the past two weeks.

"Yeah, he did. And I am excited, nervous, anxious and scared out of my mind. I just don't want to mess up this opportunity."

"Nah, you're not going to mess this up. You got this. You know how I know?"

"No, tell me."

"Because you're one of the best things that's ever happened to that school, babe. You're creative, you love those kids, they love you, you've proven over and over again how valuable your take on curriculum development is, and you deserve a chance to put your all into something that fulfills you. Phillip knows that. You just gotta know that."

"I'm getting there. This helps."

"Good. So, then, I guess I have to institute some tough love for us both and tell you to get up and take a shower so that you can officially start your day."

"Mmm," I whined. "You're right, but can I just lie here another fifteen minutes first?"

"I'm not going to say no to that. So yeah, let's do it. In fifteen, you go take a shower, I'll start making breakfast and then after we eat, I'll help you with your pitch."

"You don't have plans today?"

"Nothing more important than this, so no."

"Okay, sounds like a plan, then."

I closed my eyes again and breathed in his scent. Even sweaty from dancing and partying last night, he smelled the best kind of way you could smell on a sleepy Sunday morning. He smelled like mine.

When I cut off the shower, I immediately caught the distinct aroma of Nick's hard work in the kitchen. Wafting through his apartment was the sweet scent of bacon, pancakes, eggs and, maybe best of all, French roast coffee. The man knew how to speak my food love language, that was for sure. I stepped out of the tub, grabbed my black satin robe from behind his bathroom door and tied it around my waist. Then, before I left the room, I slid my shower cap off, smoothed my hair down, lathered my arms and legs with the little bit Nick left me of the lotion on my side of the bathroom counter, and swept a tiny dollop of moisturizer up my face in small circles.

This had been my routine on the few occasions when we had a chance to stay inside on the weekend, and it was definitely something I realized I missed when we were on the outs. Maybe some routine things weren't so bad after all, I thought, because this just made me feel like I was home.

Finally done, I walked downstairs and set my eyes on a beautiful sight: Nick, in just his gray boxer briefs, standing at the stove flipping a pancake. I mean, if there was a picture for incidental seduction in the dictionary, this would have been it. I closed my mouth to keep from drooling.

"Hey, there."

"Hey," I responded, stepping into the kitchen. "It smells sooo good in here."

"It better. I'm in here working hard for you."

"Well, it's very appreciated." I leaned in and kissed him, and he slapped me on my butt, slyly positioning his hand right at the hem of my robe so that he could feel my skin with his touch.

"Pancakes should be ready in five minutes, and that's the last thing that's on the menu. I made some coffee for while you wait."

"Mmm, bless you." I reached over the counter and grabbed the mug that had become my favorite over the past three years—a soup bowl–size white coffee mug with gold trim. In it, he'd prepared my coffee just as I liked it: black with two teaspoons of sugar.

"Good?" he asked, just as I took my first big gulp.

"You have no idea how good."

"Ha, well, I probably have some idea from the satisfied face you just made."

"Well, that face is not just for the coffee. I do have a very sexy man standing in front of me cooking with just his boxer briefs on. That, plus this coffee, is a pretty satisfying situation."

I moved in closer to him, invading his space and placing my body in between him and the stove.

"What are you doing, Jenny?" he asked, laughing.

"If I recall correctly, someone once had me in a similar spot cooking for him. And he decided that he wanted me more than the food."

With my best attempt at recreating our fifth date, I turned off the stove, slid the pancake pan away from the burner and pulled Nick into a deep, sensual kiss, licking his teeth and tugging at his upper lip.

"That guy was smart and right. Because the last thing I want to do right now is eat this food. I'd rather eat—"

Just then, I cut myself off, realizing that maybe those words weren't as sexy coming from me as they were from him. Nick found it hilarious.

"No, no, finish it! What were you going to say?"

"I mean, I don't want to eat you, so maybe that doesn't work exactly, but you get the point." I pushed him just slightly and bit my lower lip in anticipation while he just continued chuckling.

"Yeah, yeah, I get the point. But see, this goes to show that you can't be like me!"

Nick stepped back into me and slapped my butt

with the spatula, distracting me just enough to swing me around and wrap his arms around me from behind. In my ear he whispered, "I'm the only one who does the eating around here, remember that, okay?"

"Whatever!" I laughed and breathed into the weight of his body around me. I must have gotten really comfortable, though, because just then, the biggest growl came from my belly, interrupting the silent, intimate moment we were having in each other's arms.

"Seems to me like you want this food more than you think, anyway. Or at least your stomach does."

"Okay, okay."

"I'm just saying. That sounded like a grown man's grumble."

"Nick!"

"It's all right, baby. Don't worry. Chef Nick is at your service."

With another slap on my butt cheek, he moved me to his left side so that he could resume making the pancakes. I stood there drinking my coffee, blatantly looking him up and down, as he flexed his muscles for me in jest. One thing I noticed in my staring was that Nick might have stopped our fun because of my stomach rumbled, but it certainly wasn't because he'd wanted to—poking out of those gray boxer briefs was another hard spatula just aching to be let free.

"Why don't you start making your plate while I finish up?" Nick sort of ask-told me. "Because I promise you, if you keep looking at me like you are, you're going to end up with a surprise in this kitchen.

Now, I'm trying to be a gentleman and make sure you are properly fed before you work, but you have ten more seconds of looking at me like a piece of meat before I bend you over this counter."

Knowing he was very serious, I took my cue without another word, put down my coffee and grabbed two plates out of the kitchen cabinet above the sink. I figured I might as well make both our plates since he'd done all the cooking.

"Do you want everything?" I asked.

"You know I do." I wasn't quite sure if he was speaking about just the food, but I obliged and began piling spoonfuls of eggs and bacon on our plates.

Just as I finished and started bringing our plates to his dining room table, Nick flipped the last pancake over and brought them to the table, too. I couldn't remember the last time we ate in the dining room and not just in front of the TV on his couch, so things already felt different.

"All right, tell me all about this pitch. I've got weeks to make up for, but I'm here now." Nick sat down next to me and piled three pancakes high onto his plate. But even as he began eating, his focus stayed on me.

"Well, I met up with my coworker Felicia recently, and after talking to her, I'm pretty sure what I'm going to pitch is a promotion to a dean of students' position, coupled with me going back to grad school to get my master's degree. I feel like this would allow me to use my experience and creativity to help overhaul the delivery of instruction/education to the students, and then I can pull from my psychology degree to make sure it's based in cognitive behavioral therapy."

"Damn, babe, that's perfect for you."

"But... I also have to convince Phillip that I can take on something like this before I get my master's. That's the part of the pitch I need to work on still."

"Oh! Well, that's my favorite part. I get to help you prepare for bragging on yourself today? Is that what you're telling me?"

"Yeah, I guess so," I said, giggling at the way he turned the whole thing around to something that felt more positive than I did at first.

"Bet. So, today's not really going to be work at all, then. I'm ready." Nick forked a huge stack of pancakes into his mouth and winked at me. After he'd finished chewing, he made one more declaration for the morning. "But just so we're clear, I still plan on having my reward/dessert later."

Honestly, he probably could have had me right then and there, but he was right—I needed to stay focused for now. I had four days left to get myself ready for my pitch. And Nick and I, once again, seemed to have a lifetime to go.

Chapter Sixteen

At 6:05 a.m., my phone alarm stirred me out of my sleep with the all-too-familiar horns in French Montana's "FWMGAB." It had been my alarm clock song since I first heard it; there was nothing like loud, melodic horns and a rapper telling you to "get a bag" as motivation for waking up in the morning. Especially when it was to go to a job you weren't super fond of.

Usually, it took me until about the second verse before I forced my eyes open, crawled out of bed and began my daily routine. This morning, though, I dismissed the alarm before French Montana even started rapping. I was in a great mood, so, for once, I didn't need his usual coaxing. I did, however, quickly notice that while I was still wrapped in Nick's dark charcoal bed sheets, he was nowhere to be found.

Rolling over to face where his body should have been, I saw a folded note on his pillow instead.

Hey, babe. I had an early meeting this morning but didn't want to wake you. You looked like you needed your rest. Not tooting my own horn or nothing, but maybe you were a little worn-out after yesterday, ha! Anyway, I hope you have a great day. I did some more work on your proposal, too. It's on your laptop. Love you, Nick.

"Wow," I thought, sitting up and reading the letter again. So, this was why Becs left notes for Oliver, because with this one small gesture, Nick had already made my whole day. And it was only just starting.

Clutching the note to my chest with a huge smile on my face, I lay back down to daydream for a second, reminiscing on yesterday's perfect day. After breakfast, Nick and I spent the entire day together, and it was everything I'd been wanting again in our relationship. He had always been a supportive boyfriend, so the idea of him helping me with my proposal wasn't all that different, but yesterday, it was combined with hours of intimate conversation, sexy time and fun moments when we just laughed with each other about everything from bets on Lakers versus Warriors to who was more in the wrong between Nina and Darius in *Love Jones*.

On top of that, we had dinner at an actual restaurant after we picked up my laptop and some work clothes from my apartment. At some point while we were working on my proposal, we both decided that we didn't want to cut the evening short, so we made sure that I had what I needed so that I could stay at Nick's place last night.

It was kind of wild, when I thought about it, to see how much things had changed in the past forty-eight hours. As late as Saturday evening, I wasn't even sure that he would come to my party or that we would be together anymore. But then he did, and that led to the best conversations we'd had in years and honest talks about what we both needed from the other. We hadn't solved everything in one fell swoop, but we were well on our way. And I loved that for us.

Another five minutes passed as I snuggled in Nick's bed in bliss before the horns started blaring again from my backup alarm.

"Okayyy," I said aloud to no one, and then I stepped out of the bed and let the song play while I got ready to take my shower.

Walking past the outfit I'd picked out last night, I realized that I must have been drunk on love or something, because while it was super cute, I had a feeling it wasn't going to be highly functional for the day. In my love haze, I'd pulled out a brown blazer, white button-down shirt and acid-wash jeans. The clothes weren't the problem, however. It was the shoes! For some reason, I'd chosen pointed-toe blush

heels with an ankle strap and a bow on the back…
to teach a bunch of third graders. It was something
Reagan would love, but I was worried I'd be in deep
pain by the end of the day.

But I guess beauty requires that sometimes. Plus,
it wasn't like I had much else in the way of options;
it was either those shoes, my heels from the party
or the sandals I kept at Nick's to walk around in his
apartment. So, ankle-strapped heels it would be. In
a weird way, if was also kind of kismet, since this
was hopefully the start of the week that I'd convince
my vice principal to create a new job for me. In the
words of Reagan, that deserved heels.

After I was properly moisturized and dressed and
had taken about fifteen minutes to do my hair and put
on my daytime makeup, I headed downstairs and saw
my laptop open on the dining room table. I checked
my phone and saw that I had ten more minutes before I needed to leave, so I sat down to see what Nick
had done overnight. To my surprise, he'd added three
more slides to my PowerPoint presentation—all focused on what having a dean of students would look
like at Kendall Elementary.

On Nick's slides were the following:

Why Kendall Elementary needs a dean of students
- It will make school more enjoyable for the
  students by creating proactive strategies to
  build student and school culture.

- It will mean more support for teachers on the disciplinary end.

- It will help spread effective classroom management strategies throughout the school.

- It will allow the principal and vice principals to focus on staff development, curriculum implementation and academic culture.

What this will look like

- A focus on instilling a sense of responsibility in the students by developing and sharing clear rules and providing daily opportunities for success

- Observations and one-on-ones with teachers at least once a month to provide feedback and collaborate on behavior management strategies

- Staff meeting workshops

- Assistance tracking and responding to behavior interventions

- Celebrating students when they exhibit one or more of our school's values and live up to the shared expectations we establish

Why I deserve the job

- As the current third grade–level chair, I have already started doing some of the work required for this role to be successful, such as:

◊ Organizing several parent engagement activities, including potlucks, gallery walks and door-decorating competitions

◊ Building and maintaining extremely positive relationships, not only with the parents in my class, but with parents across the entire grade level

◊ Conducting weekly grade-level meetings and setting expectations and action steps for the upcoming week, as well as observing each lead teacher and following up those observations with coaching meetings and feedback

• My background in psychology uniquely qualifies me to incorporate what I've learned into practices that the school can manage, and my experience in teaching for the past eight years gives me a great understanding of what support other teachers will need in order to realize the goals of enhancing the culture of the school and facilitating positive behavior management.

I read Nick's slides in complete awe. First, it showed just how much he'd been listening to me when I talked about what I wanted to do and why. But also, it was the perfect complement to what I'd already included in the PowerPoint, and it summed up the remaining items in a concise and easy-to-understand way. I could see why he was the golden guy at work!

With little time left to spare, I packed my laptop into my work bag, put on my high heels, made sure to lock Nick's door and headed to the train station. Thankfully, it was only a couple blocks away, and because it was not quite 7:00 a.m., there were just enough seats left for me to grab one. Once seated on the train, I pulled out my phone to text him thank you.

You are the most amazing boyfriend, I typed, a smile emanating from my face as if he could see me.

Nick replied almost instantly.

Ha-ha, tell me more.

Me: Thank you for adding to my slide deck, first of all. I don't know how much longer you spent on that last night, but it was just the last pieces I needed.

Thank you also for the note, the weekend...for just being you.

Nick: :) You're welcome, babe. We're just getting started on this new version of us.

Hey, before I forget, do you have plans tonight?

Me: No, not really.

I looked up just long enough from our conversation to make sure that I hadn't missed my stop. Two more stops to go, I noticed, and then brought my attention back to my phone.

Nick: Okay, good, meet me at Palmer Alley at 6:00?

Me: You got it! I'll be there.

Nick: All right, babe. Have a good day. I love you.

Me: I love you, too, Nick.

The train pulled into my stop as soon as I pressed the Enter button, so I hurried up and put my phone back into my work bag, stepped off the train car and made my way to work. I was officially ready to take on the day, find out what country my students would pick next in the now very popular globe game we'd started at the beginning of the school year, and then meet up with my man after.

I couldn't ask for anything more.

By the time all my students ran out of class, their book bags flying behind their backs, I was already getting excited for the evening. It would be another three hours before Nick and I met up, however. So, I used the time in between to clean my classroom, prepare plans for the week and look over my PowerPoint presentation again. I had a feeling that I was going to be reviewing it until my meeting on Thursday; I just really wanted to make sure I made a good enough case for why Kendall needed the position and why it should be for me.

When it was almost time for me to meet Nick, I suddenly realized that I had no idea which restaurant he intended for me to go to. Palmer Alley, the pedestrian mall running in between the city's popular, mixed-use development called CityCenterDC, not only featured a three-block radius of high-end fashion stores like Dior, Gucci and Louis Vuitton, but it also included several restaurants. So, I wasn't sure if he wanted me to go to Fig & Olive, Del Frisco's Double Eagle Steakhouse, DBGB Kitchen & Bar, Piccolina, or any of the other eateries in the walkway.

I pulled my phone out of my bag to call Nick as I walked up to our meeting location. With the sun having already set, the walkway was lit up with silver and gold lights and trinkets that almost looked like large snowflakes. The way they reflected off the glass buildings made me feel like I was surrounded by twinkle lights. And then in the middle of the walkway stood Nick, three dozen blush peonies in his hand, his smile competing with the lights for what shone the brightest.

Immediately, my mouth fell open, and I stopped myself from dropping my phone in shock.

"Nick?" I asked, still somewhat in disbelief. "What a-are you doing?"

"Well, I was waiting on my beautiful girlfriend

to show up," he said, his smile still lighting up the entire area. "But now I'm standing here, just taking in the incredible woman before me. I mean, wow, you are stunning."

It was amazing how Nick could still make me blush after all this time. And maybe because I'd missed the feeling for a while, it seemed that much more important to feel my cheeks burning, my heart fluttering and my breath quickening without him so much as touching me. In fact, we were still about five steps away from each other when my feet stopped moving. There was my man, the finest thing in Palmer Alley (including me), with his fitted black turtleneck and gray plaid dress pants barely hiding his muscular frame. It was probably a good thing that I didn't see him before work, because I might not have wanted him to leave.

"Thanks, babe. But what is all this?"

Nick moved in closer to me so that he could give me the flowers. He also lightly brushed his lips over mine, the kind of sweet hello kiss that would normally simply feel endearing but tonight inspired a host of tingling sensations in my body.

"I just wanted to bring you flowers tonight, that's all." He paused and gave me a sly smirk. "I can still do that, right? Now that I'm back in your good graces?"

"Of course," I responded. With my composure starting to come back to me, I was suddenly also very aware of all the other people in Palmer Alley staring at us as if they expected a...

"Wait, is this a proposal?" I blurted out, interrupting my own thoughts. "Are you proposing to me right now?"

"Ha-ha, nah, babe. I really did just want to get you some flowers. You know, I'm trying to listen when you tell me you want more romance and desire."

"Oh, okay," I said with an internal sigh of relief. Not that I didn't want to marry Nick, but I'd always sort of wanted an intimate proposal that took place with just the two of us, since ultimately it would be just us going on a life journey together. As magical as Palmer Alley was, something about him asking me to marry him there felt too much like a movie scene and not reality. "Well, I love the way you listen."

I leaned into him and kissed him slowly, dragging my hands down his back.

"And I love the way you thank me. Whew." Nick breathed deeply and straightened his back before continuing. "How about we head to the restaurant before I forget why we're here and hail us a cab home?"

Home. I caught his use of the word without the qualifier of it being his or mine, but ours, and clutched my peonies close to my chest. Nick might not have been proposing just yet, but hearing him speak about our future was a great reminder that that was absolutely what I wanted. I wanted to build a home and a life with this man.

"Speaking of restaurant," I said, trying to jolt myself out of thinking too far into ideas of our future so that I could enjoy the present. "Where exactly are we going? I forgot that I never asked."

"Oh, ha, literally right here. We're going to Fig & Olive."

The upscale Mediterranean restaurant was indeed right in front of us, which gave me yet another instant of relief that I didn't need to walk another three blocks in my heels. I'd managed to keep them on all day, but it was certainly time to sit soon.

Nick and I turned to head into the restaurant, beautifully decorated in earth tones and wood and marble decor, and again, I felt all eyes on us. I guess the fact that I was carrying three dozen flowers in my hand made us stand out.

At the front of Fig & Olive, just past and to the right of the revolving glass and black doors, a blonde woman waited to greet us.

"Ooh, are we celebrating something tonight?" the hostess asked.

"Nothing in particular," Nick quickly answered and winked at me. "She deserves the world, so I figured some flowers are but a small part of that."

"Oh my God," she screeched. "How dreamy is he? And do you have a brother?"

"Sadly, they are all taken and in California," I responded with laughter. "Many have asked."

"I bet they have! Well, happy for you, honey. We should all be so lucky."

I turned and looked at Nick, who was grinning

like a Cheshire cat. Normally, I would have messed with him about such a blatant compliment, but the hostess was right—I was lucky.

"I'm going to hear about this all night now, I see," I said, turning back to her. "But you're right, he's worth it." I took Nick's hand in mind and squeezed it to let him know I meant every word.

"Well, let's get you two lovebirds to your seat. You can follow me."

Up the winding stairs we went to the top floor and into a cozy area with gray-and-orange seating.

"Have you two been here before?"

"No, we haven't," Nick answered.

"Well, I hope you have an amazing dinner, then. Your waiter will be with you in a few."

Nick and I both sat in the booth part of our area, choosing to sit next to each other rather than across from the other. We used the chair for my peonies instead.

"I think she wanted you, babe," I said to him once I was certain that the hostess was out of earshot.

"Well, she can look, but I'm all yours."

"Damn straight."

A few minutes later, our waiter showed up to ask what we wanted to drink and eat. For Nick, it was scotch neat and a hanger steak with baby kale; for me, rosé sangria and a salmon burger with mixed greens and balsamic dressing. We also ordered three of their signature crostinis to share.

"So, how was your day?" Nick asked as we waited for our food.

"Honestly, it was pretty good. I was a little worried about these heels, but even that worked out. The kids were on the best behavior today, so I didn't have to run around as much as normal. And…since it was Monday, they picked their new country to explore."

"Aw, man, this is my favorite part, too. What did they pick?"

"Brazil! One of the kids shouted 'Carnival!' when Kevin's hand landed on it. It was so cute."

"Wow, they know about Carnival at eight?"

"I know, it's wild what they already know sometimes, but…internet."

"Oh, yeah, I guess that's true. My parents still had us using Encyclopædia Britannica when I was ten, so I don't know that life."

"Babe, we were not using the encyclopedia. Don't lie!"

"I'm serious!"

"You're telling me you weren't using AOL in 2000?"

"I mean, we had it, but you know my parents—they're old-school trying to raise five boys. They wanted us spending as little time as possible on the internet because someone told them about the AOL chats. I was definitely still cutting pictures out of the encyclopedia for school," he said laughing.

"Babe!" I was full-on laughing by now. "Okay, that's also not what you were supposed to be doing.

Magazines, Nick. That's what magazines were for when we were kids."

"Hey, I used what I had." He shrugged.

"I hear ya. Well, what about you? How was your day?" I braced myself for Nick's normal reluctance to talk about work. We'd had a weekend full of intimate conversations, but I knew work and his feelings about it were usually a sticking point.

"You know, actually, it wasn't so bad today. The only frustrating thing was that I had a guy come to my office at around five o'clock to see if I could help him with some budget recommendations for his department. I told him, straight up, 'Bruh, it's 5:00 p.m. I can help you tomorrow, but I have somewhere to be in an hour, so that's not happening today.'"

"Whoa," I said, shocked not only to hear that Nick told someone at work no, but that he was going into details about something frustrating during his day with me.

"Babe, do you know this guy had the nerve to say to me, 'Well, I know you're usually here late, so I didn't think five o'clock was a problem for you'?"

"Oh, no."

"Yeah, it took everything in me not to respond, 'It's not a problem for me—it's very clearly a problem for you.' I kept my cool, though, because, you know, I can't really be the aggressive Black guy in the office. So, I just said, 'Look, man, like I said, I have somewhere to be tonight. But I can help you tomorrow. Best I can do.'" He shrugged like I imagined he'd shrugged to the guy in his office as well.

"And?" I was engulfed in the story now and hoping I didn't have to go down to Nick's office at some point and stare down whoever this guy was.

"And he dealt with it. He just said, 'All right, man, I appreciate that.' I could see he was butt hurt, but he'll be aiight."

"He better damn be." I was starting to get heated thinking of someone possibly disrespecting him at work.

"It's all right, babe. He is. You're cute when you're angry for me, though. Might have to tell you these stories more often."

"Please do, actually. I love hearing it. And I'll try not to get too worked up."

"Nah, keep that energy. I like it." He winked at me, letting me know he might not have just been talking about my enthusiasm for making sure his coworkers respected him. "Actually, that reminds me. Something else I wanted to talk to you about was finding a therapist for me. I like what yours is doing for you, and I'm thinking, you know, maybe it's time a brother talks to somebody, too."

"Babe. Yes, I love that. I can ask Diane for recommendations for Black men. It's not going to be easy at first, though, just being honest."

"Yeah, I figured. But it'll be worth it."

Okay, talk about sexy! Forget gray sweatpants— a Black man in therapy who was working on his communication was about the most attractive thing I could think of. Before my mind could start wandering off too far to think about sultry ways that we could celebrate this journey of his, our waiter came back to the table with our drinks and crostinis. Not a moment too soon.

"By the way, are you staying with me again tonight?" Nick asked, taking a sip of his scotch.

"Mmm-hmm." I'd already started shoving a smoked salmon crostini into my mouth as he asked me, but really, it wouldn't have mattered. My only answer was yes at this point. *Yes, I'm staying with you tonight. Yes, I'm the happiest woman in the world.*

"Okay, good. Guess we'll need to stop by your place and pick up some more clothes. Maybe a few outfits to be safe."

Yes, I'll stay as long as you want.

"That works for me," I said, finally done chewing.

"Good, good. Me, too."

Back in Nick's apartment (ahem, *home*), I unpacked my overnight bag and began hanging up the outfits I'd brought from my apartment into his closet, stacking each day's outfit on a single hanger to ensure that it was easy for me to pick it out when I needed it. For the week, I'd packed a couple pairs of slacks (one a mustard yellow and one a sort of rust color), a couple blazers and oversize sweaters, and the outfit I wanted to wear for my pitch on Thursday: dark blue ankle pants, a black-and-white-striped blouse, with my new Christian Louboutin heels—Reagan's birthday gift. Probably most importantly, I brought a couple pairs of some cute flats with me as well: my mixed Ankara-print LeyeLesi oxfords and my brown ModCloth flats with the heart-shaped polka dots.

To the untrained eye, it might have looked like I was trying to move in. But honestly, as pretty as my heels were, I didn't want to be stuck wearing them all week while trying to wrangle third graders into being kind, productive human beings. That today worked was a miracle all on its own. Plus, Nick did say to pack a few things. Once everything was in its place, I turned and saw Nick already lying in the bed. Had I taken that long?

"Wow, you're already ready for bed?"

"Babe, I washed my face, moisturized, changed out of my work clothes and have been lying here watching you meticulously put everything up for the last five minutes. You can't say 'already,'" he laughed. "But don't worry, I'm not going to bed without you."

"Ha-ha, well, thanks for the kind gesture after maybe insulting me? Hmm, I may have to rewind the tape to see."

"Never, babe, just an observation of how incredibly detailed you are."

"I'm a teacher! Who cleans her room every day

and puts all the kids' items back into their appropriate places before I leave work."

"I know. And now I see why."

Nick smiled his infectious smile again, and I nearly melted from across the room.

"You're done now, though, right?"

"Yes, yes. I am done," I said, rolling my eyes. "Let me just go to the bathroom and freshen up and I'll join you in bed."

"Okay, I'll be here waiting."

I walked to his bathroom and immediately went to my side of the counter, once again noticing that Nick's side was fairly bare—but only because he always used my stuff. One day, I supposed, it would be *ours*. With that thought lingering nicely in my head, I went about my nightly routine—washing my face; brushing my teeth; rinsing with mouthwash to make sure that when I woke up in the morning, I didn't have morning breath; and wiping down all the important body parts. The last thing I wanted was for Nick to feel frisky in the middle of the night and I wouldn't be ready.

Ten minutes later, I walked back into Nick's bedroom and saw him lying down with his body facing the bathroom. This time his smile had a touch of nervousness with it, and I almost asked why until I looked at the rest of the bed.

There, in front of him, in my spot, was a black ring box that had been opened to reveal a beautiful halo-cut diamond ring.

"Hi," he said as my mouth dropped all the way to the floor.

"Nick—"

"So, here's the thing. I've been working more hours and saving up for the perfect ring the past six months. But I hate that in that time, I had you questioning my love for you, my absolute desire for you and my commitment to this relationship. I will never do that again."

I took a few more steps and lingered at the edge of the bed, my hands covering my mouth and tears beginning to fall from my eyes. Just a few hours before, I'd thought he was proposing, he told me he wasn't, and now here he was, asking me to marry him in the exact intimate way I wanted. What a roller-coaster ride!

After a few moments, I sat on the bed and braced myself to talk. Nick sat up at the same time, facing me with the ring still in between us.

"It wasn't just you, though," I said once I could finally move my mouth to speak again. "I had a lot of things I had to work on in myself, and am still working on, but therapy is helping a lot. You weren't wrong to feel like I was comparing us to other people. I was—maybe not intentionally, but I was."

"And you weren't wrong to ask me for more."

"Yeah." It felt really good to hear him say that.

"So, now I'm asking you." He picked up the ring box and cupped it in his large hands. "I don't want to spend the rest of my life with anyone but you. Will you marry me?"

Tears streaming down my face, I leaned in and kissed Nick, holding his face close to mine. And then, with a big breath, I inclined my body back, looked him in his eyes and said the only thing I could say—the only thing I'd been able to or wanting to say all night.

Yes.

Yes, to everything, just yes!

Chapter Seventeen

"So, you see, Vice Principal Phillip, what I'm proposing is mutually beneficial. Kendall is already seen as a groundbreaking elementary school with its willingness to use innovative models to teach Black and Latino kids so that they excel in their studies and in their personal lives. A dean of students position builds on this legacy."

Thursday's pitch to my vice principal came a lot faster than I expected, but there I was, standing in front of him with my accountant-approved Power-Point deck, attempting to give the presentation of my career. We'd scheduled the meeting during my planning period, so I knew I had forty-five minutes to present, answer any questions he had, secure a yes, text everyone what happened and go to the bathroom before my class came back. If I'd calculated everything correctly, that meant I had fifteen minutes for my actual presentation, and a quick look at my watch reminded me that I was coming up on minute thirteen. I continued.

"That means, yes, it will have a focus on behavior management, which I believe is critical to assisting our kids in their personal growth. But also, I'd make sure that we have a focus on celebrating the students, not only for their academic successes but also for being brave enough to show up and be their little, human selves—with particular consideration given to their experiences as Black and Latino youth."

I clicked the mouse to the last slide in my PowerPoint deck and took in one last breath while also trying to see if I could gauge my vice principal's reaction to my presentation so far. I'd already covered all the basics—what a dean of students would do for Kendall Elementary, how it would help the teachers and the students, why Kendall needed the position specifically, why I was the best person for the job even though I didn't have my master's yet, and why they should pay for me to get my degree. Now, I was trying to bring it all full circle, with the hopes I'd left him in such awe, he'd have no choice but to say yes. The whole time, however, he sat in his chair and watched me stoically.

"In conclusion, creating a dean of students position at Kendall—and putting me in it—not only benefits the students emotionally and socially, but it will also provide our teachers with additional behavior management resources and tools that they can actively implement in the classroom. And it will give teachers and the vice principals more time to focus on instruction, observation, and feedback, therefore improving students' learning on an everyday basis. Lastly, it will continue to position Kendall as a cultural example in the public charter school space in DC and across the nation."

When I finished, I smiled at Vice Principal Phillip, knowing that I'd officially given it my all, covered everything I've discussed with Felicia and Nick, and that I was prepared for whatever came next. I ended the presentation and sat down in the chair across from him, waiting with bated breath for him to speak. He sighed deeply, flipped his pen through his fingers a few times and leaned forward before ever saying a word. It was torture, but I kept my composure.

"Well, Jennifer, that…" He paused again, drawing out his reaction even longer. "Was a fantastic pitch. I can see that you've thought about this a lot. To be honest, I need talented teachers like you, who the students love and relate to, so, I would hate to lose you from the classroom. But you've also made an excellent case here for why we need you as our dean of students even more."

Finally, I released my shoulders, unclenched my jaw and breathed a sigh of relief. If Vice Principal

Phillip was saying what I thought he was saying, it was going to take every relaxed bone in my body not to jump out of my chair, kick off my Louboutin heels like Patti LaBelle when she gets excited in the middle of her performances and run around the room screaming and thanking God.

I swallowed deeply and asked, "Wait, does that mean—"

"It does," he said, interrupting me. "I think this is a great idea, and I'm in full support of you. Now, I'm going to have to convince the higher-ups to approve the position, and you have to do your part by getting accepted into a master's program for education. But as far as I'm concerned, we should start looking for a new teacher for next year, because I want to see you in this role. I think we need it, and you're the best one for the job."

"Vice Principal Phillip! Thank you, thank you, thank you." Unable to control my happiness any longer, I leaped out of my seat and almost ran over to give him a hug. I was in midair with my arms stretched wide when I caught myself and threw out my right hand to shake his instead. "Genuinely, I really appreciate you supporting me on this. You won't regret it."

"I already know."

Vice Principal Phillip stood up, buttoned the middle of his suit jacket closed and shook my hand again.

"Great job again, Pritchett. You did good. I am meeting with Principal Carter early next week, and

I'll be sure to mention this to her and let you know what she says."

Having heard all the words I needed to hear, I turned toward the door, my cheeks burning from smiling so hard. I couldn't believe it had actually worked. After all the work I'd done, it was finally starting to feel like I was on my way to doing something where I felt challenged again, in all the best ways.

I speed walked back to my classroom, the sound of my heels clicking on the floor echoing in the hallway. I had ten minutes left before class started and still needed to do two more things on my list before little kids walked through my door.

By the time I made it to my desk, where my phone was hiding, however, my body suddenly reminded me that maybe going to the bathroom should be my priority. It was almost like my body had been instinctively holding in my need for the restroom until the pitch was over, but now that it was done, I had to get to a toilet quick. I scooped up my phone and practically sprinted back down the hallway to the teachers' lounge and then into the restroom. Then I quickly unzipped my pants, wiggled out of them and sat down just in time. Figuring that I might as well multitask, I unlocked my phone and went straight to the top three text chains that mattered—one with Nick, one with my girls and one with my parents.

To the girls: Agghh!! I did it. Phillip says he completely supports me on creating the dean of students' position. It's lit!

To my parents: Guess what? My vice principal loved the idea! Your daughter might be a dean of students next year :)

And to Nick: Baaaaaaaabe. We did it! I'm going to be Kendall Elementary's first dean of students. Aghhhh! Thank you so, so much.

Immediately, my phone began pinging back in response.

Reagan: Yessssss! I knew you'd kill it.

Robin: OMG! You're such a rock star! Tell us everything!!

Rebecca: Yes, yes, yes!! And you know what this calls for, right?

Reagan: Shots!!

Robin: Shotssss!!

Rebecca: Should we meet at Jenny's tonight? Celebratory Nacho Thursday? I could probably get there by 6p.

All I could do was smile and laugh. My group of friends really did know how to celebrate each other; I don't know how I ever got caught up in comparing myself to them and thinking that any of that mattered when our friendship had always been about unconditional love and support from the jump. More to unpack during therapy, I figured.

Next, I heard from my parents. Well, to be exact, it was my mother texting on both their behalf: Jenn, your dad and I are so very proud. We can't wait to hear all about it. Call us when school is out.

I was typing in my responses when my phone rang. I happily saw that it was Nick.

"Jenny, you did it," he blurted out before I could even say hello.

"Thanks, Nick," I said in a whisper, not wanting someone to come into the restroom and hear me on the phone. "It's not a completely done deal, but he basically told me, 'Go apply to a master's program and get in, so we can do this.'"

"Of course, he did," Nick said in full voice, not needing to whisper on his end due to having his own office, and, well, not being in the bathroom. "You were more than ready for this, so I had no doubt. In fact, you know what? We're celebrating tonight. I'll cook. I just need you to be my sexy sous chef while you tell me the whole story of how things went down. I don't want you to leave any detail untouched. That work for you?"

"It sounds perfect." I caught myself smiling again and then realized my time was running out and I needed to get back to class. "Oh, wait, I need to go, Nick. But I love you. See you tonight."

"I love you, too, Jenny."

We hung up, and I went back to texting my parents and then Reagan, Robin and Rebecca. Of course, in the few minutes I was talking to Nick, the girls had continued texting and were almost completely done finalizing plans for the evening until Robin realized I never responded to the initial question.

Robin: Jenn, are you still there?

Me: Yes! Sorry guys, Nick called. Can we celebrate tomorrow night? He wants to cook for me.

Rebecca: Ooh, of course! We can't compete with that.

Reagan: Say less. We'll be there tomorrow!

Robin: Ha-ha, yeah, girl, get your celebratory meal from your man. Nacho Friday works for me.

Me: Thanks, ladies :) You three are the best...someone bring some tequila, because I'm running low.

Reagan: We got it!

With seconds to spare, I finished in the bathroom, washed my hands and sprinted back to my classroom. I'd just sat down and was starting to catch my breath when the first three students walked in.

"You okay, Miss Jenn?" asked Caresha.

"Oh, yeah, I'm good. Thanks for asking, sweetheart. I just tried to run in these shoes," I said, pointing to them so that she could see.

"That doesn't sound fun," she said, scrunching her face.

"I gotta tell ya, it is not."

"But they are really cute!" Jared screamed out from the back of the room. He and many of the rest of the students had made their way back into the classroom and were starting to settle into their desks.

"Yes, they are, Jared. And my friend Reagan would love that you noticed that."

"My mom talks about wanting red bottoms all the time," he said, his face beaming with joy as he spoke. "I don't know why she doesn't just paint them. Did you paint yours, Miss Jenn?"

"No, they came like this. But can I tell you a secret?"

His eyes opened really wide as he waited. "Mmmhmm."

"I kind of wish they were blue to match my pants."

Jared and a few of the other students busted out laughing, giving me the exact reaction that I'd hoped for. If there was anything I was going to miss next year about not being in the classroom, it was going to be this—the times I had an opportunity to make my students laugh and feel supported with just a few small statements. I only hoped that my career switch would enable other teachers to do the same and make it that much easier for me to do it in a nonclassroom setting.

Walking into Nick's apartment, I immediately caught a whiff of chicken, sausage and maybe soy sauce or sesame oil. It was a very pleasant surprise, since I didn't realize that Nick would be home when I arrived.

"Mmm, something smells so good!" I called out to him, slipping my shoes off at the door.

"Join me in the kitchen so you can taste it."

I didn't need much coaxing in that area. I quickly made my way toward him, very briefly stopping to wash my hands, and then perched my body directly next to his.

"What's this?" I asked as Nick twirled some of the noodles onto a fork for me to taste.

"It's called Pancit Bihon. My mom used to make this for us whenever we had something to celebrate, so I figured I'd try my hand at it for tonight."

"Nick!" I was so touched. Nick had just cooked breakfast for us days before, but this felt different. He was cooking a meal that meant something to his childhood, and all I could think about was the idea of him making this meal for any kids we'd have when it was time to celebrate with them. I didn't want to start crying all over him, though, so I pulled myself together and refocused my thoughts. "Okay, tell me what's in it."

"Honestly, a little bit of everything." He silently

encouraged me to open my mouth so that he could place the fork inside as he explained it to me. When the noodles hit my tongue, it was an explosion of flavor, and that only continued as I chewed and he described what I was tasting.

"So, it has rice noodles, chicken, Chinese sausage, garlic, onion, cabbage, carrots, celery, achuete powder, oyster sauce, soy sauce, sesame oil and salt and pepper. Once it's done cooking, I'm going to add some scallions and lemon on top."

"Wow. It's soooo good," I said, finishing up and savoring my bite. "Is this what I can look forward to as Mrs. Carrington? Home-cooked Filipino meals from my super sexy husband?"

"Ha-ha, maybe so."

"Mmm, what a lucky girl I am, then."

"Not luckier than me." Nick slapped me on my butt and winked at me, and my whole insides fluttered within. "Why don't you go get comfortable? Dinner should be ready in ten minutes."

"Wait, I thought I was going to be your sous chef. And I'm out of clothes, babe! Technically, I was supposed to go back to my place tonight."

"Oh, right," he said, scrunching up his face to let me know he didn't like the idea of me going back home. "I started cooking with my mom on FaceTime, and before I knew it, we were almost done. Sorry. But this works anyway, because I want to hear all about what happened, and I couldn't have paid attention like I would want while trying this recipe for the first time."

"That's true. But next time!"

"Definitely next time…now, as for clothes, I have a closet and dresser full of them that you can put on."

"That's true. I guess soon enough it will be what's mine is yours, right?"

"Ha-ha, yeah, something like that."

I ran up the stairs to Nick's loft bedroom and quickly picked out one of his T-shirts and a pair of his basketball shorts to change into. On me, they looked ginormous, and not exactly exuding sex appeal, but they had his scent, so I could totally see myself not wanting to take them off. I looked at myself in the mirror before heading back down and decided, no, I couldn't be that much a tomboy—not tonight. At the last minute, I slipped out of the shorts, choosing to rock his shirt and my panties as my only attire. Nick might have prepared a delicious dinner, but I had ideas about dessert.

"Babe, is the food ready?" I asked, walking back down the stairs.

"Yep." Nick's mouth hit the floor when he saw me step into the dining room, my legs making an entrance before the rest of me did. "And you better start telling me about the pitch before I completely change my mind about what tonight's meant to be about."

I sat down at the table and relayed the entire thirty-five minutes, word for word, as we ate. The stark contrast to the woman I was a few months before who believed she didn't have any story to tell wasn't lost on me. That woman had been so incredibly sad, and now I was once again not just happy for myself but also for everyone around me. It was no longer about how I couldn't compete with what they each had going on; it was about being content in my own story and excited for what was next for me.

Nick ate the whole detailed story up, asking me for specific details, like, "What did his face look like when you mentioned the master's degree part?" and "How did you handle it when he tried to fake you out and act like he wasn't going for it?" Between his excitement, my newfound confidence in my own life story and the amazing food that we were eating, I wasn't sure if the smile on my face would ever disappear.

Chapter Eighteen

The main ingredients that you need for Nacho Thursday—or Friday—are as follows:

- an overwhelming amount of tortilla chips
- ground beef sautéed with taco seasoning
- strips of chicken
- chopped tomatoes
- green onions
- shredded Mexican cheese
- fresh salsa or pico de gallo
- sliced limes
- black beans
- tequila

- margarita mix
- lots of laughter
- and even more love

Since I was hosting this week's Friday version, I made sure to stop at the store on my way home from work and pick up the items I didn't already have, which mainly were all the fresh ingredients, since I hadn't been home in almost a week. Thankfully, my students were practically angels on this day, so I was able to leave work by 4:00 p.m. (almost unheard-of on a Friday afternoon!), go to the store and make it home in time to straighten up my apartment and make three pans of nachos—one beef, one chicken and one beans only—before the girls arrived. I even had a chance to change into more comfortable clothing, choosing a white T-shirt that I tied at my waist and a pair of loose-fitting green-and-white pedal pushers that I'd purchased while shopping with Robin.

For the final bit of preparation, I pulled out four margarita glasses from my kitchen cabinet and the leftover margarita mix from the last time Nacho Thursday took place at my apartment and brought the glasses, the mix, the pans, a filled ice bucket and the sliced limes to my living room. Once all that was finished, I sat back into my couch and closed my eyes for whatever time I had left before madness and loud laughter would consume my space.

In the quiet, I had time to reflect on all that had

occurred in the past two and a half months. I'd gone from feeling incredibly lonely and boring, comparing everything about myself to my friends, and now it wasn't as if everything was perfect, but I could see the progress. I'd finally opened up to the people closest in my life about how I was feeling, as embarrassing as it was, and that led me to an amazing therapist who was helping me to process where those thoughts were coming from. And her practical advice of leaning into my friends' strengths helped me to figure out what I wanted to do with my career and bring a little spice back into my relationship and, most importantly, I no longer felt as if I was on the verge of tears at any second. And I was engaged!

Oh, crap. I sat up, suddenly realizing that I hadn't told Rebecca, Reagan and Robin about the engagement yet. It had been five days since Nick proposed and I'd said yes—a lifetime when it comes to not telling friends and family you're engaged, especially in the social media era—but we'd been in our own little cocoon all week. And I hadn't wanted to interrupt that, not even by telling my closest friends. We didn't even tell our parents until the next day, choosing to simply go to bed as fiancés and bring the world in later.

Well, I guess tonight will be celebratory in many ways.

Within a few minutes, I heard a familiar rhythmic pounding on my front door.

"Let us in, Ms. Dean of Students!" shouted Robin.

I jumped up off my couch and headed to my door,

already laughing at their antics. When I opened the door, Rebecca launched a ton of confetti into the air and the three of them began rapping the chorus to "Act Up" by the City Girls. In the haze of the confetti, I also saw they had at least twenty balloons with them, a cake and two bottles of tequila.

"Wow, you all are out of this world! Come in, please!"

"Aht, aht, you have to dance us in," exclaimed Reagan as the other two kept dancing and rapping.

"Ohhh, my bad. You got it." Still standing with my door open, I joined them in their silliness, booty bumping with Robin and doing my best high-pitched imitation of the rappers from Miami.

As promised, the three of them danced their way into my living room, transitioning their song to a simple refrain of "ayyyeees" and exclamations of their joy for me. Robin placed the bottles of tequila in the ice bucket on the coffee table, Reagan repositioned the pans of nachos so that the cake sat in the middle and Rebecca undid the balloons so that they floated individually, filling up the living room.

"Jenny, we're so excited for you!"

Robin was the first one to stop partying and grab me for an extended hug with a tight squeeze. "I know what this means for you," she whispered, and I had to hold back tears from falling down my face...but good ones this time.

It was Rebecca who noticed my ring first, though. As Robin and I were hugging, she grabbed my hand, swung me around and, with her eyes and mouth wide open, waited for an explanation. Reagan and Robin didn't understand what was happening at first—until they followed Becs's eye line to my ring finger and immediately started screaming.

"OMG!! OMG!!" Reagan shouted.

"When did this happen?!" Rebecca asked.

"On Monday." I scrunched up my face, bracing for the onslaught for how long I'd taken to tell them.

"Monday?!" Robin asked with about the amount of shock I was preparing myself for.

"As in five days ago?" Reagan interjected.

"Like, one, two, three, four, five…" Becs added, counting the numbers on her fingers dramatically.

"Yeaahhhh. But don't hate me! We've literally only told our parents so far."

"And anyone who's seen you walking around with this gorgeous ring!" Robin pointed out.

"Well, not really. I haven't worn it out yet, because I wanted to make sure you three knew first."

That helped calm them down enough that I could tell them the proposal story without further dramatics. All three found their places in my living room near the coffee table. Reagan sat perched on the edge of the right side of the couch, and Robin plopped onto the floor in between the couch and the table and instantly began mixing tequila with the margarita mix. Rebecca sat on the opposite side of the coffee table, leaving me with the left side of the sofa to fill.

Robin took a large gulp of her drink and then revisited the conversation.

"Okay, that's actually really sweet of you," she said. "Now, we want all the details. Tell us everything."

And I did. For the next ten minutes, I told them how we'd been together basically since the birthday party and how he'd been working more hours to pay for the ring, so that was part of why he was so tired lately and we'd lost our spark. I also told them how we'd talked and both admitted that there were things we'd each done wrong in terms of communication—him in shutting down and letting that affect how open and vulnerable he was with me, and me in not honestly telling him what I needed and instead trying to seduce our way back to some sort of "normalcy." Finally, I told them how he'd tricked me the whole night on Monday, making me believe he was proposing and then not doing it, only to surprise me when I walked out of his bathroom and saw the ring sitting on the bed.

By the time I was done going over each detail, they were all staring at me with giddy eyes, barely even touching the three pans of nachos I'd laid out on the table for us.

"Jenn, this makes me so, so happy!" Robin, of course, was the first one to say something. "I mean, I still want to shake him for what he put you through, but I love the two of you together, so this is good!"

"Well, from what I hear, we can thank Becs for

some of this," I said, turning to her. "And thank you, by the way, for whatever it is that you said."

"You're welcome, but honestly, I didn't have to say much. He already had the ring. So, it was mostly me being like, 'Well, you got her an engagement ring for a reason, so what are you doing?'"

I laughed as I popped a beef-filled nacho in my mouth.

"And then, when I saw that he came to the party, I was maybe drunkenly telling him that it was about time he manned up and showed up for his girl."

"Now, that's more like it," Reagan interjected.

"Speaking of the party," I said, turning to her now. "Nick and I weren't the only couple reuniting there. I believe I saw you and Jake sneaking out of there at some point."

"Oh, you mean when you were having sex on the sidewalk?" she asked, giving me a face that clearly said, *mmm-hmm, I saw you, too*.

"Whoa! Okay, one—this is not about me anymore, and two—you saw that?!"

"Yes, Jenny, if you can see me, I can probably see you."

"Touché…but don't deflect. What's going on there?"

"Sooo…" she started and then took a big gulp of margarita. "We're back together."

"Thank God," we all said in unison.

"What?!" she asked, flabbergasted.

"I mean, no, really, our lives are less stressful when you two are together," added Rebecca.

"Okay, okay, I get it. Say less."

"So, what does this mean," I asked. "Long-distance again?"

"Actually, maybe only for a little while. I talked to my boss about letting me open a New York office, which wasn't a hard sell for a women's magazine. And they were down for it. They're looking into We-Work spaces for me to move sometime in the spring."

"Um, the party was less than a week ago!" I pointed out. "When did all this happen?"

"Yeah, and you're engaged, too, so clearly a lot can happen in a week."

"Agh! Okay, fine." I shut my mouth briefly with another chip.

Thankfully, Robin took over for me.

"So, obviously we're happy for you, Rae, but what's different this time? You all just broke up a few months ago, and it wasn't only because of the long distance."

"You're absolutely right. It wasn't. It was lack of communication, me still trying to wait for everything to be perfect and him still letting his fears stop him from asking of me what he wanted. Basically, the night of the party and then the next day, we put everything on the table. Like, okay—I want to be with you. So how do we make this happen?"

"Okay!" I shouted, liking what I was hearing.

"And you know, it didn't hurt that we were both very unhappy seeing the other on a date with someone who wasn't us."

"I knew that was going to put a fire in your butts," said Robin.

"It definitely did! So, I guess that's one thing I can thank the date pact for."

"Ohhh, the date pact," Rebecca said, rolling her eyes.

"We know. You didn't like it."

"It wasn't that I didn't like it, I just felt that it was a waste of both your times," she countered. "But hey, if it got you and Jake to have an open and honest conversation, then I'm here for it."

"Well, speaking of date pact, I may have to start a new one in January, because my bosses agreed to my London move."

"What has happened in this week? I feel like I'm never going into a Nick cocoon again!" I looked down at my phone and saw that he was texting me, almost like I'd conjured him up.

Nick: Does around 10pm sound good?

Me: Yeah, we should probably be ending about then.

Nick: Okay, see you then. Love you.

Me: Love you, too.

I returned to the conversation in front of me, completely unable to hide my growing smile.

"...plus, you knew I was already thinking about it," Robin continued, but then she paused upon seeing my face. "Ooh, that's a happy Nick face! I like this."

"Whatever, don't make me blush...and thinking about it, yes, but I didn't know it was in the works."

"If that happened with that beautiful brown skin of yours, we'd really know Nick performed miracles... and anyway, it wasn't in the works...and then it was. And I wanted to say something at the birthday party, but I chickened out. I'm so excited about this opportunity, but I have to admit, I'm nervous about leaving everyone and going across the ocean for more than a couple months."

"That's fair," I said, moving closer to her.

If I was completely honest, the last thing I wanted was for my best friend to move across the ocean, too, especially as Reagan was going to New York as well. But the reality was that we were all heading for new and exciting horizons in our thirties, and that was always inevitably going to look different for us. For some friends, this meant navigating new babies and marriages; for us, at least for now, it was going to mean making sure we maintained our friendship no matter where we lived. We'd made the vow to each other at the birthday party, and now we had to keep it.

"But like Rae said before, we'll just have to become frequent flyers."

"And thankfully Zoom is a great invention," chimed in Rebecca.

"Wait, you're not leaving, too, right?" I asked her.

"Ha-ha, no, you're stuck with me for now."

"Whew! Okay, because my little heart can only take so much."

"Yes, and that super sensitive heart is why you were the one I was most worried about leaving," admitted Robin. I could see her eyes getting a little puffy as she held back a few tears. "But I'm so proud of the work you've been doing in therapy and just in advocating for yourself. Now I'm seeing a Jenn I never saw before—one who is still the best kind of friend but also to herself."

"Robiiiiiin, you can't say that kind of stuff and expect me not to cry!"

"I'm sorry! But it's true." She wiped her face and sat up straight. "Okay, enough of that. Let's talk logistics, because you all are saying that you're coming to London, but I plan on flying back for every bridal obligation you have for this wedding. I'm talking shower, bachelorette, engagement party, all of it. And Rae, you already know that I'm coming in town when you move to New York. And Becs...wait, Becs, you've been awful quiet. What's going on in your life these days?"

"So, actually, Olly and I are thinking of trying to have a baby."

"Whaaaaaaat?!" we all screamed in unison.

"You and Olly as parents? OMG!" Reagan added.

"You're going to be such a good mom," I said.

"It's not a done deal yet, you guys. But it's something we're at least talking about. I have an appointment to get my IUD removed in a few weeks, actually."

"Okay, that is beyond talking about it," remarked Robin.

"Ha-ha, okay, maybe a little more than talking… but I'm thirty-five, so you just never know how my age will play out with everything."

"What does that mean for your lifestyle?" Reagan asked.

"Well, I'm not entirely sure. But I figure that you can have the white picket fence and choose what happens behind your fence, right?"

"So right."

"I feeeeeel like…" I started and ate another nacho before continuing. "We missed one Nacho Thursday because it was the week of the birthday party, and so much has happened. So, the biggest thing this tells me is that even once Rob and Rae move, we can't miss a week!"

"Definitely can't miss a week," Robin agreed.

"Because if we do, one of you will pop up married, and then we're going to have to fight," said Rebecca.

"Don't look at me! Engaged is as far as I'm going with the surprises. I still need to get into a master's program, get Kendall to officially create this new job for me and kill it at work. I have a feeling Nick and I will need at least a year to plan for this thing… although I could see us moving in together before the wedding." The last part I let trail off my tongue a bit, feeling it out as I said it aloud and liking how it sounded.

"Okay, yes, let's go back to you. Because we still haven't heard anything about the pitch nor this little dreamy cocoon you and Nick were in this week," Robin said.

"Yes, I will tell you all everything, of course. But somebody needs to eat these nachos other than me. I can't sit here and eat three pans when I have a dress to fit into eventually."

"Oh, we got you!" Reagan proclaimed and scooched closer to the food so that she could grab a few nachos to stuff in her mouth.

"Yeah, sorry, I was just so caught up in all the news," Robin added.

We spent the next few hours eating, drinking and plotting out how we'd make sure we were all present for any future milestone occasions, starting with Rebecca's IUD removal. That was good enough of a reason for a cozy girls' night in where we watched Babs's movies, ate lots of popcorn and had ice packs and heating pads at the ready.

Just like clockwork, Rebecca started yawning about 9:50 p.m., which kicked off the cascade of yawns from Robin and Reagan and some sad acknowledgments that the night might be over.

"We just aren't spring chickens anymore, ladies,"

Reagan said, ironically while downing the last of her fifth margarita.

"Speak for yourself. I'm still the only one who's not thirty yet in here."

"All right now, you'll be thirty in a month, so let's not get too excited," said Robin. Oh, I was going to miss her snarky but loving attitude. I caught myself before I got emotional again.

"She's also the only one staying here tonight, so she doesn't have to worry about getting back home and not falling asleep in an Uber," added Rebecca.

"True! True!"

"You all are welcome to stay here!"

"No, no, I saw the way you looked when Nick texted you earlier. That was the look of a fiancé coming over tonight," said Robin.

"Mayyybbbeeeee," I said sheepishly, starting to pile the empty pans on top of each other to bring them to the kitchen.

"Mmm-hmm," they all said knowingly.

Just then, we heard keys jangling at my door and saw Nick walking in.

"Hi, ladies," he said as soon as he saw they were still in my living room.

"Oh, hiiiii, Nick."

"Yesss, hiii, fiancé."

"Ha-ha, I see she told you three." Even while he was taking off his shoes and coat at the door, his smile shone all the way to where I was in the kitchen. I could tell he was happy that they were happy.

"Uh, yeah, she better had! And we're only letting y'all get away with this five-day nonsense because of how much we love you two," Reagan said, walking up to him to give him a hug.

"She's right," added Robin.

"Trust me, I know."

His shoes and coat finally off, Nick walked all the way into my apartment, and I could finally see him in full. In his left hand were another dozen pink peonies for me. I caught his eye while washing the dishes and gave him a quizzical look. I still had three dozen at his place! But he just shrugged his shoulders and winked at me and placed them on the coffee table for when I was done in the kitchen.

"We really are proud of you for fighting for our girl, here, Nick," Rebecca said, interrupting the staring contest Nick and I were having across the apartment.

"Well, Becs, the truth is, I had no choice, really. I can imagine my life without Jenn, in theory, but there's no reality where it makes sense for me."

A series of awws rang through my apartment, and I could see Nick eating it up.

"I think that's our cue to skedaddle, ladies and gentlemen," said Robin.

"Yep, calling my Uber right now."

From the kitchen, I watched each of them pack up their belongings and head outside as their cars arrived, promising to text when they got home. And when the last one left, Nick locked the door behind them and started unbuttoning his shirt and then pants as he walked toward me. By the time he was directly in front of me, he was just in his boxer briefs, very clearly ready for action.

"Good evening, Mrs. Carrington," he said, scooping me into his arms as he plastered light kisses all over my neck and walked us back to my bedroom.

"Trying out my future last name, huh?"

"You like it?"

"I love it."

"Good."

Nick laid me down on the bed and climbed on top of me as my body melted under his.

"Because you're going to be hearing it for the rest of your life."

* * * * *

*Don't miss the next book in The Shoe Diaries
miniseries, coming October 2022!*

*In the meantime, check out these other romances
about established couples:*

Last Chance on Moonlight Ridge
By Catherine Mann

The Five-Day Reunion
By Mona Schroff

*Available now wherever
Harlequin Special Edition
books and ebooks are sold!*

#2917 SUMMER NIGHTS WITH THE MAVERICK
Montana Mavericks: Brothers & Broncos • by Christine Rimmer
Ever since rancher Weston Abernathy rescued waitress Everlee Roberts at Doug's Bar, he can't get her off his mind. But the spirited single mom has no interest in a casual relationship, and Wes isn't seeking commitment. As the temperature rises, Evy feels the heat, too, tempting her to throw her hat in the ring regardless of what it might cost her heart...

#2918 A DOUBLE DOSE OF HAPPINESS
Furever Yours • by Teri Wilson
With three-year-old twins to raise, Ian Parson hires Rachel Gray hoping she'll solve all their problems. And soon the nanny is working wonders with his girls...and Ian. Rachel even has him agreeing to adopt a dog and cat because the twins love them. He's laughing, smiling and falling in love again. But will Ian need a double dose of courage to ask Rachel to stay...as his wife?

#2919 MATCHED BY MASALA
Once Upon a Wedding • by Mona Shroff
One impetuous kiss has turned up the heat on chef Amar Virani's feelings for Divya Shah. He's been in love with her since high school, but a painful tragedy keeps Amar from revealing his true emotions. While they work side by side in her food truck, Divya is tempted to step outside her comfort zone and take a chance on Amar—even if it means risking more than her heart.

#2920 THE RANCHER'S FULL HOUSE
Texas Cowboys & K-9s • by Sasha Summers
Buzz Lafferty's "no kids" policy is to protect his heart. But Jenna Morris sends Buzz's pulse into overdrive. The beautiful teacher is raising her four young siblings... and that's t-r-o-u-b-l-e. If only Jenna's fiery kisses didn't feel so darn right—and her precocious siblings weren't so darn lovable. Maybe it's time for the Morris party of five to become a Lafferty party of six...

#2921 WHAT TO EXPECT WHEN SHE'S EXPECTING
Sutter Creek, Montana • by Laurel Greer
Since childhood, firefighter Graydon Halloran has been secretly in love with Alejandra Brooks Flores. Now, with Aleja working nearby, it's becoming impossible for Gray to hide his feelings. But Aleja's situation is complicated. She's pregnant with IUI twins and she isn't looking for love. Can Gray convince his lifelong crush that he can make her dreams come true?

#2922 RIVALS AT LOVE CREEK
Seven Brides for Seven Brothers • by Michelle Lindo-Rice
When a cheating scandal rocks Shanna Jacobs's school, she's put under the supervision of her ex, Lynx Harrington—who wants the same superintendent job. Maybe their fledgling partnership will make the grade after all?

HSECNM0522

SPECIAL EXCERPT FROM

HQN

*Stationed in her hometown of Port Serenity, coast guard
captain Skylar Beaumont is determined to tough out
this less-than-ideal assignment until her transfer goes
through. Then she crashes into Dex Wakefield. She
hasn't spoken to her secret high school boyfriend in six
years—not since he broke her heart before graduation.
But when old feelings resurface, will the truth bring
them back together?*

Read on for a sneak peek at
Sweet Home Alaska,
*the first book in USA TODAY bestselling author
Jennifer Snow's Wild Coast series.*

Everything looked exactly the same as the day she'd left.

Though her pulse raced as she approached the marina and the
nondescript coast guard station, her heart swelled with pride at the
sight of the *Starlight* docked there. With its deep V, double chine
hull and all-aluminum construction, the forty-five-foot response
boat was designed for speed and stability in various weather
conditions. Twin diesel engines with waterjet propulsion eliminated
the need for propellers under the boat, making it safer in missions
where they needed to rescue a person overboard. Combined with
its self-righting capability to help with capsizing in rough seas, it
had greater speed and maneuverability than the older vessels. The
boat was the one thing she had total confidence in. And she would
be in charge of it and a crew of five.

The crew was the tougher part. She was determined to gain
their trust and respect. She was eager to show that she was one
of them but also maintain a professional distance. Her father and
grandfather made it look so easy, but she knew this would be her

hardest challenge, to command a crew of familiar faces. People she'd grown up with, people who remembered her as the little girl who'd wear her father's too-big captain hat as she sat in the captain's chair in the pilothouse.

Did that hat finally fit now?

Weaving the rental car along the winding road, and seeing the familiar Wakefield family yacht docked in the marina, her heart pounded. The fifty-footer had always been the most impressive boat in the marina, even now that it was over thirty years old. Its owner, Kurt Wakefield, had lived on the yacht for twenty-five years.

Kurt had died the year before. Skylar peered through the windshield to look at it. Had someone else bought the boat? Large bumpers had been added to the exterior, and pull lines could be seen on deck. She frowned. Had it been turned into some sort of rescue boat?

It wasn't unusual for civilians to aid in searches along the coast when requested, but the yacht was definitely an odd addition. There had never been a Wakefield who had shown interest in civil service to the community…except one.

The man standing on the upper deck now, pulling the lines. Wearing a pair of faded jeans and just a T-shirt, the muscles in his shoulders and back strained as he worked and Skylar's mouth went dry. She slowed the vehicle, unable to look away. Almost as if in slow motion, the man turned and their eyes met. Her breath caught as familiarity registered in his expression.

And unfortunately, the untimely unexpected sight of her ex-boyfriend—Dex Wakefield—had Skylar forgetting to hit the brakes as she reached the edge of the gravel lot next to the dock. Too late, her rental car drove straight off the edge and into the frigid North Pacific Ocean.

Don't miss
Sweet Home Alaska,
available May 2022 wherever
HQN books and ebooks are sold.

HQNBooks.com

Get 4 FREE REWARDS!

We'll send you 2 FREE Books plus 2 FREE Mystery Gifts.

FREE
Value Over
$20

Both the **Harlequin® Special Edition** and **Harlequin® Heartwarming™** series feature compelling novels filled with stories of love and strength where the bonds of friendship, family and community unite.

YES! Please send me 2 FREE novels from the Harlequin Special Edition or Harlequin Heartwarming series and my 2 FREE gifts (gifts are worth about $10 retail). After receiving them, if I don't wish to receive any more books, I can return the shipping statement marked "cancel." If I don't cancel, I will receive 6 brand-new Harlequin Special Edition books every month and be billed just $4.99 each in the U.S or $5.74 each in Canada, a savings of at least 17% off the cover price or 4 brand-new Harlequin Heartwarming Larger-Print books every month and be billed just $5.74 each in the U.S. or $6.24 each in Canada, a savings of at least 21% off the cover price. It's quite a bargain! Shipping and handling is just 50¢ per book in the U.S. and $1.25 per book in Canada.* I understand that accepting the 2 free books and gifts places me under no obligation to buy anything. I can always return a shipment and cancel at any time. The free books and gifts are mine to keep no matter what I decide.

Choose one: ☐ **Harlequin Special Edition**   ☐ **Harlequin Heartwarming**
(235/335 HDN GNMP)   **Larger-Print**
(161/361 HDN GNPZ)

Name (please print)

Address   Apt. #

City   State/Province   Zip/Postal Code

Email: Please check this box ☐ if you would like to receive newsletters and promotional emails from Harlequin Enterprises ULC and its affiliates. You can unsubscribe anytime.

Mail to the **Harlequin Reader Service:**
IN U.S.A.: P.O. Box 1341, Buffalo, NY 14240-8531
IN CANADA: P.O. Box 603, Fort Erie, Ontario L2A 5X3

Want to try 2 free books from another series? Call 1-800-873-8635 or visit www.ReaderService.com.

*Terms and prices subject to change without notice. Prices do not include sales taxes, which will be charged (if applicable) based on your state or country of residence. Canadian residents will be charged applicable taxes. Offer not valid in Quebec. This offer is limited to one order per household. Books received may not be as shown. Not valid for current subscribers to the Harlequin Special Edition or Harlequin Heartwarming series. All orders subject to approval. Credit or debit balances in a customer's account(s) may be offset by any other outstanding balance owed by or to the customer. Please allow 4 to 6 weeks for delivery. Offer available while quantities last.

Your Privacy—Your information is being collected by Harlequin Enterprises ULC, operating as Harlequin Reader Service. For a complete summary of the information we collect, how we use this information and to whom it is disclosed, please visit our privacy notice located at corporate.harlequin.com/privacy-notice. From time to time we may also exchange your personal information with reputable third parties. If you wish to opt out of this sharing of your personal information, please visit readerservice.com/consumerchoice or call 1-800-873-8635. **Notice to California Residents**—Under California law, you have specific rights to control and access your data. For more information on these rights and how to exercise them, visit corporate.harlequin.com/california-privacy.

HSEHW22

HARLEQUIN

Heartfelt or thrilling, passionate or uplifting—Harlequin is more than just happily-ever-after.

With twelve different series to choose from and new books available every month, you are sure to find stories that will move you, uplift you, inspire and delight you.